Twice in a Blue Moon

THE HENRY TIBBETT MYSTERIES

ALSO BY PATRICIA MOYES

Twice in a Blue Moon

PATRICIA MOYES

AN OWL BOOK

HENRY HOLT AND COMPANY   NEW YORK

Henry Holt and Company, Inc.
Publishers since 1866
115 West 18th Street
New York, New York 10011

Henry Holt® is a registered
trademark of Henry Holt and Company, Inc.

Library of Congress Cataloging-in-Publication Data
Moyes, Patricia.
Twice in a blue moon / by Patricia Moyes.
    p.   cm.—(A Henry Holt mystery)
1. Women detectives—England—Fiction.   I. Title.
    PR6063.O9T87   1993
823′.914—dc20   93-9531
                CIP

ISBN 0-8050-2823-4
ISBN 0-8050-2948-6 (An Owl Book: pbk.)

Henry Holt books are available for special promotions and premiums. For
details contact: Director, Special Markets.

First published in hardcover in 1993 by
Henry Holt and Company, Inc.

First Owl Book Edition—1994

Designed by Paula R. Szafranski

Printed in the United States of America
All first editions are printed on acid-free paper.∞

1 3 5 7 9 10 8 6 4 2
    5 7 9 10 8 6 4
            pbk.

This book is affectionately dedicated to Robin's typewriter, without which it could never have been written.

Twice in a Blue Moon

AN INSPECTOR HENRY TIBBETT MYSTERY

CHAPTER

1

The whole thing started with Horace Prothero's letter. It arrived on a Monday morning, along with a singularly dull collection of catalogues and bills, plus a get-well card from an old school friend—not very appropriate, since I had been home from the hospital for nearly a month. The mystery was explained by the fact that she lived on a Caribbean island, and the envelope—correctly addressed to me in Kingston, Surrey, England—had been stamped "Missent to Kingston, Jamaica." My friend says that such things are part and parcel of Caribbean charm.

In any case, the communication from Battersby, Wilcox, Prothero and Golightly, Solicitors, was sufficiently intriguing to make up for the rest of the mail. It was short and to the point.

Dear Miss Gardiner,

I would be obliged if you would call on me at your earliest convenience at the above address, where you will learn something to your advantage concerning the will of your late great-

*uncle, Sebastian Gardiner. Please telephone my secretary at the
above number to make an appointment.*

Yours truly,
Horace Prothero

The address was an office in Theobald's Road.

Having heard that the legal profession in London tends to
linger over its eggs and bacon, and seldom shows up for work
before ten, I contained my impatience until nearly eleven before dialing the number.

Mr. Prothero's secretary had a clipped, middle-age voice,
which suggested that I was taking up time that she needed for
something else. However, on hearing my name she softened
slightly, and agreed that Mr. Prothero would be able to see me
at eleven-thirty the following morning.

"Please leave me your telephone number, Miss Gardiner. I
shall have to call you back to confirm the appointment."

"You will? Why?" I asked.

"Well, naturally I shall have to check with Mr. James
Gardiner. Mr. Prothero wishes to see you both together." I
gave her my number, and she rang off snappily.

I put down the telephone, feeling, like Alice in Wonder-
land, that things were getting curiouser and curiouser. It was
a beautiful spring day, near the end of March, and the daffodils in my small backyard were putting up a brave show of
color. I pulled a chair out from the kitchen–dining room of my
ground-floor flat and sat down in the sunshine to consider the
situation and its possibilities.

First, I suppose I had better introduce myself. My name, as
hinted above, is Susan Gardiner, and at the time when these
events took place I was twenty-seven years old, unmarried, an
orphan, and recently discharged from hospital after undergo-
ing a hysterectomy.

I was, for the moment, unattached romantically. I had been living for nearly two years with a boyfriend called Paul, who really doesn't come into this story at all—because for some reason my hysterectomy seemed to revolt him out of any sexual desire, and I came home from the hospital to find a note pinned to the proverbial pin cushion informing me that he had moved out and gone to live with a blonde called Betty. I was also unemployed.

When I left school, with quite respectable O levels but no thought of even attempting any A's, my parents predictably suggested a secretarial training. However, I strongly objected. I hate offices and all that goes with them. I like living in the country, and the only thing I was ever really good at was cooking.

I begged and cajoled, and finally got my way. My family was not rich, but my father insisted that if I was serious about going into the catering business, it was worthwhile to make sacrifices to have a really good training. So I was enrolled at a first-class hotel school in Switzerland, near Lausanne. (My French was quite good, which helped.)

I had a wonderful time. As well as hotel management and cookery, I learned to ski and sail, and every day I blessed my parents for sending me there, because I knew it wasn't easy for them. Dad was in insurance, but by no means at the top of the ladder. I knew that the cost of my training meant skimped housekeeping and an absence of holidays. However, when I was in my last year and due to graduate just before Christmas, I got a letter from Mum saying that she and Dad had decided to fly out for the diploma-giving ceremony, and that we would then go up into the mountains, all three of us, for a holiday.

You must have read about the crash in the papers. Nobody ever found out exactly what happened, because there were no survivors. The weather at low altitudes was lousy that day, and something must have gone wrong with the altimeter—or so the inquiry concluded. Anyhow, instead of landing at Geneva, the plane hit a mountainside—and that was that.

I came back to England with my diploma and quite a lot of insurance money—as if that helped. Anyhow, I sold my parents' house in Ealing and took this flat in Kingston—mainly because it was on the ground floor and had a small garden and a view of the river. My eventual aim was to find work at a really good hotel in the country, but common sense told me that some experience in London first would stand me in good stead. So I began job hunting.

Even with a diploma like mine, you start pretty low down in the hotel business, and I did the usual stints in every department you can think of in some of the best London hotels and restaurants. By the time I was twenty-six, and had acquired Paul, who was a fairly successful commercial artist, I decided that I was ready to move on to bigger and better things—and that's when the doctor discovered this tumor on my womb and decided that the whole thing must be whipped out.

Fortunately, it was benign—what an expression, as if the wretched thing was sitting there grinning kindly at me—so at least it wasn't going to kill me, for which I was profoundly thankful. I was enjoying my lonely convalescence, and starting to think about finding work, when Prothero's letter arrived.

Now, I knew very little about my great-uncle Sebastian. I never remember meeting him, although I'm told I did so a few times when I was a baby. All that my parents said about him was that he had become extremely eccentric as he grew older, after the death of his wife. They had had no children, and Great-uncle Sebastian became more and more of a recluse, living by himself in the big old house he owned near Holland Park.

The house, I gathered, was just about his only asset. He

had bought it when he got married nearly fifty years ago—in those days, property in that part of London was still relatively inexpensive. It was a large place, with a garden and seven bedrooms (if you count the servants' quarters), a vast drawing room, and all the fixtures. The snag was that it had only two bathrooms and an antiquated basement kitchen—but even so, it would be worth a fortune today. If my great-uncle had only sold it, he could have lived in comfort somewhere smaller—but he wouldn't. Instead, he progressively shut up various rooms until he was living in what used to be the morning room, where he installed his bed and a gas ring for cooking. And it was there he had died, at the age of eighty-three, while I was in hospital for my operation.

I did know, vaguely, that I had a distant cousin called James. He was the grandson of Uncle Sebastian's brother George, but the family had moved to Canada when I was still a small child, and we had completely lost touch. George Gardiner and his wife were both dead, and I hadn't given a thought to their grandson until Prothero's letter came. I did remember Dad remarking that both James's parents had been killed in a motor accident, but it hadn't occurred to me that he—the unknown James—and I were Great-uncle Sebastian's only living relatives; but of course we were.

Horace Prothero's secretary rang me back that afternoon to confirm the appointment, and so at half-past eleven the next morning I found myself in the offices of Battersby, Wilcox, Prothero and Golightly in Theobald's Road.

I had expected the offices to be Dickensian—dark, gloomy, and untidy—but I couldn't have been more wrong. The outside of the building was pretty venerable, but inside it had been completely modernized. The receptionist sat at a semicircular Plexiglas desk in the outer lobby, which had white-painted walls and a lilac carpet. She checked my credentials on what looked like a minicomputer (what's wrong with an old-fashioned engagement book?) and then favored me with an empty, dazzling smile.

"That's right, Miss Gardiner. Mr. Prothero will see you right away. Mr. Gardiner has already arrived." She pressed a button on her desk, and almost at once a very young, trim brunette appeared through the swinging plate-glass doors that led to the main office.

"Marjorie, please take Miss Gardiner to Mr. Prothero's office." The telephone on the receptionist's desk began to ring—or rather, to buzz discreetly. She picked it up and lost all interest in me.

"This way, please, Miss Gardiner," said Marjorie.

She led me through a big open-plan office, also decorated in lilac and white, where secretaries sat at eerily silent word processors and fax machines. It was ages since I had been in an office—not since my father's death, actually—and I missed the cheerful clatter of typewriters and the shrilling of telephones. At the far end of the room were several white-painted doors, one of which bore a discreet, brass-framed card reading MR. HORACE PROTHERO.

"Miss Gardiner," said Marjorie, opening the door and standing back to let me through.

The contrast was staggering. I found myself standing in exactly the sort of old-fashioned solicitor's office I had been expecting from the beginning. A dowdy, middle-age lady—undoubtedly the one who had spoken to me on the telephone—sat at a small desk tapping away on an ancient office typewriter. The furniture was all heavily Victorian—dark wood and burgundy leather upholstery—and the walls were lined with bookshelves holding fraying leather-covered tomes. The main desk was enormous, and entirely covered with papers. And behind it, rising to his feet and smiling welcome, was Mr. Horace Prothero himself.

6

"Good morning, Miss Gardiner. Delighted to see you. Pray take a seat." Horace Prothero was a big, heavy man with white hair and a beard and moustache to match. He wore pin-striped trousers, a waistcoat, horn-rimmed spectacles, and a gold fob watch. "You know Mr. James Gardiner, of course?"

Until that moment, I had been so overcome by the difference between Mr. Prothero and his outer office that I had hardly noticed that there was anybody else in the room. Now I became aware that there was a man in his thirties sitting, his back half toward me, in one of the two wooden-armed mahogany chairs facing Prothero's desk. The chairs were of the old-fashioned revolving type, and now the young man swiveled round to face me, as he got to his feet.

"Cousin Susan," he said, holding out his hand. "I suppose we may have met in the cradle, but I'm afraid I don't remember it."

"Nor do I," I said. "But it's nice to meet you now." We shook hands, and I had a chance to take a good look at my long-lost distant cousin.

He was certainly an attractive man. Not especially handsome, but with a thin, interesting face, very dark brown eyes, and fair hair. His handshake was firm, but all the same I had the impression that he was nervous. Well, so was I. Neither of us knew what to expect.

Horace Prothero was beaming at both of us in an avuncular way. "Sit down, sit down," he said, and I almost expected him to add "my children." We all sat, and Prothero began sorting through the heaps of documents on his desk.

"Now, where was I? Where's   . ? Ah, yes, here it is." He extracted a very legal-looking paper, hung about with red ribbon and sealing wax. He looked up at us over his spectacles, which had ridden down toward the end of his broad nose. "The last Will and Testament of Mr. Sebastian Gardiner, deceased."

James and I exchanged a glance, both amused and nervous. Prothero went on. "You probably know that your great-uncle was not a wealthy man when he died. I was his friend of many years—toward the end, I think I may say that I was perhaps his only friend. For years I had begged him to do the prudent thing—to sell his house and take out an annuity—but he would have none of it." He sighed, then beamed again. "Well, as it turns out, Mr. Gardiner, that was lucky for you. I won't bore you with the legal phraseology, but this very simple will states that you are to inherit whatever monies and chattels Mr. Sebastian Gardiner had in his possession at the time of his death, together with his property at 106 Holland Park Crescent." He beamed at James over his horn-rims. "The monies are, I fear, negligible, but of course the property is worth a great deal. Even in its present dilapidated condition, I should value it at well over half a million pounds."

James did not smile back. Leaning forward with his hands on the desk, he said, "And what about Susan? What does she get?"

I confess I was wondering the same thing. Surely Prothero wouldn't have summoned me there just to tell me that I was to inherit nothing. Besides, there was that phrase about "something to your advantage."

I was surprised to see that Horace Prothero was beaming again, this time in my direction. "Miss Gardiner," he said, "also receives a bequest. It is not, of course, in the same category as yours, Mr. Gardiner, but it is by no means worthless. By no means." He paused and cleared his throat. "Miss Gardiner, you inherit Mr. Sebastian Gardiner's other property."

"His other property?" I repeated. "I always understood he didn't have—"

"Few people knew about it," Prothero conceded. "He

bought it some years after his marriage. His wife, apparently, had some idea of running it as a hobby, but it never came to anything."

"But what is it?" I was getting exasperated.

"It is," said Prothero, "a small country hotel—or inn is perhaps the more accurate word—situated just outside the village of Danford, in Essex. It is called, for reasons that I do not comprehend, The Blue Moon."

"Well, what's happening to it now?" I demanded. "Who's running it? Did it ever make any money? What—"

Prothero held up his hand. "One moment, one moment, young lady. As I said, I am possibly the only person who knew about Mr. Gardiner's ownership of The Blue Moon—except for the present tenant-landlord, of course. He paid a small rent to Mr. Gardiner, which enabled my old friend Sebastian to eke out his unhappy existence. Apart from his old-age pension, it was his only source of income in his final years. However, Mr. Tredgold, the incumbent lessee, is an elderly man, and will retire as soon as the property is handed over formally to you. He confided to me over the telephone that he only kept the place on out of concern for old Mr. Sebastian. I fear that the property is very run down and for years has never made even the barest living for its tenant. My advice to you, Miss Gardiner, is to sell it for what it will fetch. The site, I believe, has a certain attraction, being alongside a small river, the Dan. However, that part of the country is becoming steadily more industrialized—which may be your best hope of getting a reasonable price for it."

Prothero took off his glasses, polished them, and stood up, indicating that the interview was over.

"My secretary, Miss Turnbull, will be in touch with you both, to settle legal details. So nice to have met you."

Miss Turnbull stopped her tapping for long enough to favor

9

us with a brief nod. We shook hands with Mr. Prothero and a moment later found ourselves out in the main office and back in the modern world.

While waiting for the lift in the corridor outside, James smiled a little shyly and said, "Well, Cousin Susan?"

"Well what?"

"I think," he said, "that we both need a drink. Not to mention a spot of lunch afterward. What do you say?"

"I'd love that," I said.

A few minutes later, sitting at the bar of a frowsty pub round the corner, I raised my glass of white wine in a toast, saying "Congratulations, Cousin James."

"Thanks." He took a sip of Scotch. "Now, let's drop this 'cousin' business. Tell me about yourself."

I gave him a rough sketch of my life to date, including the hysterectomy. I'm not quite sure why, except that after Paul's reaction, I felt it was something rather shameful that I had to admit to right away. Then I said, "And what about you?"

"Not much to tell. I was born here, of course, but brought up in Canada. I went to school and college there, and then went into business."

"What sort of business?"

"Oh—financial. A friend of my father's was a stockbroker, and he found a place for me in his firm. Nothing grand—more or less an office boy, really. But I was able to learn a lot. My father and mother were killed in a car crash twelve years ago, soon after I started work. After that, there was nothing to keep me in Canada. So as soon as I felt I knew enough about business to survive, I came back to England."

I was surprised. "So you've been over here for years?"

"Eight, actually."

"You never looked us up—came to see us?"

"I didn't even know what part of England you lived in," James protested. "I did look up John Gardiner in the London telephone directory. There are about ten pages of them. Anyhow, your parents didn't live in London, did they?"

"Well, sort of. Ealing. We were in the book—but I see what you mean. Needles in haystacks."

James said, rather slowly, "The only member of the family I knew anything about, really, was Great-uncle Sebastian."

"Oh?" I was surprised again. "You were in touch with him then?"

"That's putting it rather strongly." James smiled and took a sip of his drink. "I visited him once or twice, and sent Christmas cards. The old dear was quite ga-ga, as you probably know."

"Did *you* try to persuade him to sell the house and take out an annuity?" I asked. I hadn't meant to sound bitchy, but there must have been an edge to my voice, because James laughed.

"And throw up the chance of a valuable legacy? D'you think I'm crazy?"

I must have looked a bit shocked, because he laughed again. "Come on, Susan. Don't look at me like that. Yes, to tell you the truth, that's exactly what I did. It was terrible, the way he lived in that great house. Sordid and degrading. The legacy aspect simply didn't occur to me. But I was no more successful than old Prothero. So after a bit, I gave up visiting and just stuck to Christmas cards."

"Did he ever mention the other place—The Blue Moon?" I asked.

"Never. Not a word. In fact, he didn't mention anything very much, poor old soul." He looked at his watch. "Let's get out of this dump and get a decent lunch somewhere. Strange as it seems, I have to be back in the office at three to meet a client." He slid off his bar stool and handed me down off mine. "Have you any preference as to eateries?"

"Not really."

"Then what about The Orangery?"

"What about it?" I laughed. The Orangery is almost certainly the best and one of the most expensive restaurants in London. I didn't mention that a couple of years earlier I had done a stint there as a very junior kitchen hand. As a matter of fact, I hadn't said anything to James about the hotel school—just that I'd gone to Switzerland to "finish" and had taken various temporary jobs in London afterward. "It's a lovely idea, but we haven't got a reservation."

James was hailing a taxi. As it pulled up, he turned and smiled quickly at me. "They know me," he said. "Jump in."

They did know him. They gave us a table right away, and for a while we just concentrated on the lovely food. Then, over coffee, James said, "I have to go in a few minutes. When shall I see you again?"

"I—I don't know. I suppose when Prothero's secretary calls."

"Look here," he said. He flicked a finger at the waiter for his bill. "When are you planning to go to Essex and look at this pub of yours?"

"I hadn't even begun to think about it."

"Well, think now." The bill arrived. James glanced at it with a casual expertise that I recognized as the mark of a frequent diner-out, then laid a platinum-color credit card on it. "Think of a day next week, and I'll come with you and look the place over. If you'd like me to, that is," he added, almost shyly.

"I'd love it. I was rather dreading going alone."

James signed the credit slip and repocketed his card. "Name the day, then."

"Tuesday?"

"Tuesday it is. Give me your address, and I'll call for you. You'd better make the arrangements with the landlord yourself."

"Of course I will. But you mustn't call for me—I live out in Kingston. It's in the wrong direction. I can easily—"

"Just give me the address. I'll be there at ten."

He scribbled my address into a small notebook, then got up and escorted me out. "I'll shove you into a cab, then I have to rush. Taxi! Ah, there we are. In you get. Good-bye, Susan. See you Tuesday."

I took the cab as far as Hyde Park Corner—a short ride. I knew I could get a bus home from there. I wasn't absolutely certain what I thought of my newfound cousin, but he was certainly not somebody you could ignore. Not by a long chalk.

CHAPTER

2

At five minutes to ten on Tuesday morning, I was trying hard not to peek from behind the curtains in my living room to see James arrive. I needn't have worried. At three minutes to, there was a cheerful hooting outside, and I saw a very elegant little Ford Escort convertible, gleaming white with black leather upholstery, pulling up outside the house, and James getting out of it. I was out of the front door before he reached it.

The weather was fine, but windy, with white clouds scudding across the pale-blue sky. The forecast had mentioned the possibility of showers, so I had put on a blue waterproof parka over my jeans and shirt. I was amused to see that James was dressed almost identically, except that his parka was red, and he was wearing a pale-blue sweater over his open-necked shirt. He grinned at me.

"You listened to the forecast too, I see."

"Yes."

"Well, don't worry about the car. Just push a button and the hood goes up. Hop in."

As he threaded his way expertly toward the M25—the ring-road motorway around London—James said, "Did you tele-phone? I mean, are we expected?"

"Oh, yes. It was rather odd."

"How do you mean, odd?"

"Well, for a long time there was no reply. Then at last a man answered the phone—he sounded about ninety, and with such a thick East Anglian accent that I could barely under-stand him. Finally, I gathered that if I wanted Mr. Tredgold—that's the present landlord—I'd have to ring a different number. I thought it was funny because I called at half-past twelve, when the pub must have been open for lunch."

"But you did finally talk to Tredgold?"

"Yes, I got him on the other number. He sounds like a nice chap. He said he'd meet us at the pub around noon today. I gather he's more or less stopped opening at lunchtime."

"Well, Prothero did warn us—"

"I know. But I didn't realize things were in such a bad way. I don't suppose I'll get much for it. Oh, well." I turned to a more cheerful subject. "What about the Holland Park house? Any nibbles?"

"Not what you could call nibbles, exactly. But I've put it in the hands of several agents, and they sound interested. It's in pretty bad shape, of course, but the land is worth a goodish bit on its own." He broke off to swing out and pass a lorry that was lumbering ahead of us. "Still, I'm glad I don't need the money right away, because it may take time."

Thanks to James's expertise, we made good progress, and before too long we hit the motorway heading for the East Anglian counties.

A little anxiously I said, "I hope the exit to Danford is marked. I know it's beyond Chelmsford, but I'm not absolutely sure which—"

James looked at me sideways. "Shame on you, Susan. You haven't done your homework."

"Well, I know how to find The Blue Moon once we get to Danford. At least, I think I do. Mr. Tredgold gave me directions."

"Consider yourself lucky that I took the trouble to look it up on the map. You'd probably have missed the exit."

His pompous tone annoyed me, but I couldn't think of anything appropriate to say. I mean, he was quite right. So I withdrew into a somewhat huffy silence. I couldn't help being pleased, though, that when we came to the turnoff, Danford was marked on the signboard, as large as life. So I wouldn't have missed it.

Once off the motorway, our progress slowed down considerably, as we wound our way along leafy lanes sweetly scented with may blossom and through small villages where country buses ambled at leisure, and motor-driven agricultural implements blocked the road, taking it easy at ten miles an hour. At last, a glint of water appeared across the fields to the left of the road, and I said, "That must be the river. The Dan. It's rather pretty country, isn't it?"

As I made the remark, the sun went in and the sky darkened. A couple of minutes later it began to rain.

As James had said, it only took the push of a button to raise the roof of the car and another to bring the windows up. All the same, it was not the happiest introduction to Danford. By the time we got to the village, the rain was coming down in blinding sheets. It was still only half-past eleven, and with the aid of frantically sweeping windscreen wipers we could see an attractive-looking half-timbered inn standing right on the village street with a car park alongside it.

With some difficulty, James read the inn sign. "The Golden Goose. What do you say to nipping in for a drink? We've plenty of time."

"An excellent idea."

James pulled up at the entrance to the bar. "You go in," he

said. "I'll park the car. No sense in both of us getting drenched."

The bar was delightful. There was a log fire burning, even though the day was not all that cold, and horse brasses glinted from the dark oak beams. The long mahogany bar shone with polish, and there was a brass footrail, lamps with red shades, and a big bowl of fresh daffodils and catkins. Corny, I know, but very welcome on a rainy day in early spring.

There were no other customers—just a florid-faced elderly man in shirt sleeves and a checked waistcoat, reading a newspaper behind the bar. I presumed he must be the landlord. He looked up as I came in and put down his paper.

"Hello, there. Come on in. What a day!"

"It was fine when we left London," I said, shaking the rain out of my hair. I hoisted myself onto a bar stool.

"That's April for you," he remarked with the air of a philosopher. "What can I get you?"

"My—my friend is just parking the car. I think I'll wait until—"

"Fine, fine. No trouble." He looked at me rather curiously. "We don't get that many visitors from London. Not on weekdays. The main road is on the other side of the river, as you know."

For some reason that I couldn't really analyze, I decided not to give him the information he was fishing for. I said, "We were just driving through, and the rain came down and—"

At that moment the door swung open again, and James appeared, pushing the door with his behind as he stripped off his sodden parka.

"Real East Anglian rain," he said. "Have you got yourself a drink, Susan?"

"Not yet. I was waiting for you."

"Well, sir, what's it to be?" The landlord was all affability. James had that effect on people.

James perched on the stool beside mine. "Susan?"

"I'll take a half of bitter," I said.

"One half coming up." The landlord was busy with beer handles. "And for you, sir?"

James grinned. "I'm driving," he said. "A tomato juice will be fine."

The landlord looked a trifle disappointed, but he produced the drinks, set them on the bar, and said, "I was just saying to the young lady, we don't get so many people from London, not on weekdays."

Unlike me, James seemed to have no inhibitions about telling the truth. "We're here to look at an inn called The Blue Moon," he said. Then, to me, raising his glass, "Cheers, Susan."

The landlord gave me an even more curious look. Then he said, with a sort of elaborate lack of interest, "The Blue Moon, eh?"

"That's right. I expect you know it."

There was a little pause. Then the landlord said, "Oh, yes, I *know* it. Everybody knows it."

"Not doing much business, I understand," said James.

"No, sir. Not what you'd call *business*." His emphases seemed a little odd. "Well, of course, it takes all sorts," he added enigmatically.

"Bit outside the village, isn't it?" James went on. "Down by the river, I understand."

"That's right, sir. By the river."

"I don't suppose it gives you much competition," James remarked.

"Well, no, sir, to be frank, it doesn't. This is what you might call a high-class establishment, as you can see. But there's always some who prefer . . . well, I'm sure you know what I mean, miss." He turned to me with a rather unattractive smile.

I hadn't any idea what he meant. The only thing I did know was that I was beginning to find the bar of The Golden Goose less pleasant than it had been. James, however, plowed on regardless.

"Yes, it's a very nice little place you've got here. Do you do lunches? I was thinking . . ."

"Pub fare." The landlord was plonking. "Plain, good pub fare, sir. There's the plowman's lunch—your basic bread and cheese—and hot dogs. And Scotch eggs, but I'm afraid we haven't any today, on account of it being quiet. Then there's the frozen pizza, and the tuna sandwiches. Shall we have the pleasure of your company later on, then?"

"I expect so." James drained his tomato juice. "Come on, Susan. Drink up. We should be going. How much do I owe you? Here you are." He put a fistful of coins onto the bar. "Keep the change."

"Thank you very much, sir. Ah, it's stopped raining, I see. Have a pleasant day, sir, and hope to see you again soon."

Outside, the rain had indeed stopped, and the sun was making a gallant effort to disperse the clouds. As we got into the car, James said, "What a ghastly phony place. Still, it seems to be the only hope of getting something to eat around here, so I suppose we'll have to settle for the frozen pizza." He pressed a button, and the roof folded itself away just as the sun finally struggled through. "Right. Blue Moon, here we come."

CHAPTER

3

"You go beyond the village—that's what Mr. Tredgold said—
and there should be a lane leading off to the left, just beyond
the garage." I was peering out of the car, trying to get my
bearings. "There's a turning to the left just here."

"Yes, but we haven't passed a garage," James objected. "In
any case, I think it's a private driveway."

It was. It led up to a pair of rusty and ramshackle wrought-
iron gates, secured by an ancient padlock and set in a high,
moss-grown wall. Obviously a deserted property.

Half a mile farther on, we came to the garage—really just
an open-sided shed with a tin roof, and one venerable petrol
pump—and beyond it, the promised lane.

Essex is a flat county, so when I say that the lane ran down
to the river, I don't mean it in any very literal sense. Still,
there was a slight downhill gradient as the road twisted and
turned between high hedges. Soon we spotted the shimmer of
water ahead and, roughly tacked to a tree trunk on the right-
hand side of the lane, a dilapidated signboard. In barely legible
letters, it proclaimed THE BLUE MOON, with an arrow pointing

straight downward. This was because the whole board had sagged out of position and was hanging by one insecure nail. In fact, a small track led off to the right, and James steered the car gingerly along it. We rounded a lefthand bend—and there it was. The Blue Moon.

It was not, at first sight, an alluring building. It stood foursquare and uncompromising as a child's drawing of a house—two storied, its grayish brickwork pierced by symmetrical windows, with a couple of dormer windows poking out from the roof above. The peeling paintwork on the central front door and the window frames had once been black. In front of the house there was a circular drive—now hopelessly overgrown—girding a round patch of grass. In the center of this stood a rickety post from which an inn sign still swung. The faint traces of a blue-painted crescent, presumably representing the pub's name pictorially, were just visible. Outside the door stood a gleaming BMW of recent vintage. There was no living creature in sight. James and I exchanged slightly appalled glances. Then he parked the car and we climbed out, the still-wet grass moistening our jeans up to knee height.

"Well," James remarked. "We're here."

The front door was firmly closed, but in answer to James's knock it opened at once. Mr. Tredgold must have been standing just inside it, probably watching for the car from behind the dusty window curtain. He was a small mouse-colored man with a permanently apologetic manner. He said, "Miss Susan Gardiner?"

"That's right."

"And this is . . . ?" Mr. Tredgold shot James a look full of suspicion.

"My cousin, Mr. James Gardiner."

Mr. Tredgold relaxed a little and held out his hand, first to me and then to James.

"I'm delighted to meet you both," he said. There was a

slightly awkward pause; then, with a certain amount of embarrassment, Mr. Tredgold waved an arm in the direction of the broken-down interior. As one who abandons hope, he said, "This is The Blue Moon."

"May we look inside?" I asked.

"Oh, by all means. By all means." Mr. Tredgold pulled the door wide open, and we went in.

We found ourselves in what had once been a saloon bar. The bar itself was of solid mahogany, but sadly stained by bleached rings where glasses had stood. Round it ran a footrest apparently made of green verdigris. There were one or two stools with legs of uneven length and seats polished by generations of rustic posteriors. Behind the bar, a few shelves held dusty bottles half full of unlikely liqueurs, and a couple of beer handles indicated communication with barrels in the basement—rather pretty handles, actually, made of blue and white porcelain. I touched one, and Mr. Tredgold said sadly, "They don't work, I'm afraid. No barrels, you see. We keep a few bottles of light ale and lager in the refrigerator."

"You have a refrigerator?" There was gentle irony in James's voice.

"Oh, yes. When the electricity isn't cut off. That is, when we've had enough coming in to pay the bill." Mr. Tredgold cleared his throat. "The fact is, we don't get many customers these days."

"Any reason why not?" I did my best not to sound too sarcastic.

"Reason? I could tell you the reason!" For the first time, Mr. Tredgold showed some animation. "We've always been off the beaten track, as you might say, but people used to come down the lane to find us. Then, about eight years ago, that bast—I beg your pardon, miss—that Jack Pargeter opened The Golden Goose on the High Street."

"But surely it's an old pub, been there for years," said James.

"Don't you believe it, sir. Nothing but a couple of broken-down cottages until Pargeter bought them up and did them over. All that black-and-white timbering—fake, that's what it is. All that fancy interior—horse brasses and warming pans—picked up at sales. Looks attractive, of course. Took away all our custom. And there's more to come, and worse." Mr. Tredgold's moustache bristled at the thought. "A while back, he started to spread stories about The Blue Moon. Unlucky place. Somebody murdered here. Haunted. You know the sort of thing. There's just a few locals still drop in for a beer of an evening on the way home, but—well, there it is. You can see for yourselves."

"So you haven't been making a very good living out of it, Mr. Tredgold?" James remarked.

"A good living?" Mr. Tredgold appeared on the point of explosion. "There's no living to be made here. I'm in the textile business myself, and very glad of it. Fact is, I seldom come here anymore myself. Old Matthews sees to the running of it—if you can call it that. No, I kept on the lease because of my poor old friend Sebastian—your uncle, I suppose, Miss Gardiner?"

"Great-uncle, actually."

"Well, I'll be honest with you, Miss G. I was his batman during the war—neither of us regular soldiers, of course. I was a young lad, just called up for service, and he was a Captain. A very gallant gentleman. I admired him very much. During the war, he got married—sweet lady, she was, name of Margaret—and they bought that big place in London. Property going dirt cheap then, of course, with the buzz bombs and everything.

"Well, it's funny, isn't it, how things change. After the

war, I went into textiles and did well for myself, though I say it as shouldn't. Came to live here with the wife and kids. Well, not actually here. In Medenham, about five miles away. Next thing, I heard Captain Gardiner had bought The Blue Moon. He had a landlord, of course, but he and Mrs. Gardiner came down at weekends. I always thought they'd planned to retire here, running the pub as a sort of hobby, as it were. Probably would have too, if Mrs. G. hadn't died so sudden."

"You kept in touch, then?" James asked.

"On and off. On and off. Then I read about Mrs. Gardiner's death, and they told me in the village that the landlord had given notice and left and that poor Captain Sebastian didn't know which way to turn. Seemed the least I could do to take over the lease, being semiretired myself. But I never meant to keep it so long. It was just to tide the Captain over, like. Next thing I hear is that he's in a poor way financially. Well, I couldn't let him down now, could I? By the end, I believe the little rent I paid him was all he had, besides his old-age pension.

"But I can assure you, Miss G., that now he's gone the sooner I can be well and truly rid of this place, the happier I shall be."

"Don't worry, Miss Gardiner will terminate your lease as soon as—" James began, at the same moment that I said, "Could I please see the kitchen?"

"The kitchen?" Mr. Tredgold looked at me as if I was out of my mind, but all he said was "Through here. This way. Mind the floorboards—not in tip-top condition, I'm afraid."

He led us toward the back of the building. From the bar, we went into a biggish, very shabby room with small, dirty windows through which we could just see the overgrown lawn leading down to the river's edge. From this room, he opened a door to the right.

The kitchen was huge and quite impractical. An enormous iron range, which clearly had not been used for years, glowered at us from the far wall. A big, dirty kitchen table dominated the room, and there were a couple of porcelain sinks, cracked and filthy, which would have daunted the bravest housewife.

"Is there running water?" I asked.

"Oh, yes, there's *water*," said Mr. Tredgold, as if unwilling to admit the existence of anything useful about the place. "Only cold, of course," he added with a certain satisfaction. "I doubt if anyone's used this kitchen for a matter of years. No call for it, you see. We gave up serving snacks a long time ago."

"And upstairs?" I asked.

"Upstairs?" Mr. Tredgold sounded as if I had made an indecent suggestion. "Well, you can see if you want, but I wouldn't advise it, really I wouldn't. Most of the stair treads are very dicey. But I can tell you there's four bedrooms and a sort of bathroom. Over the w.c. down here, which I didn't show you, because it doesn't work. Well." He turned to me with what was almost triumph. "There it is, Miss G. The Blue Moon."

James said, "I think Miss Gardiner will be prepared to terminate your lease immediately, so that you won't have to pay out any more. Isn't that so, Susan?"

"Absolutely," I said. I had heard an ominous rustle, such as is associated with rats on the prowl.

Mr. Tredgold smiled, for the first time. "Thank you, Miss Gardiner," he said. "Thank you. You've taken a weight off my mind, I can tell you. When can we sign the papers?"

"I'll get Mr. Prothero—that's my late uncle's solicitor—to draw them up right away. Meanwhile, if there's any rent due—"

"I've paid up to the end of the month, Miss G."

"Then we'll send you a check for anything outstanding after the papers have been signed." I smiled and held out my hand "Thank you, Mr. Tredgold."

"Thank *you*, Miss Gardiner. And Mr. Gardiner, of course.'

We walked out again onto the rough gravel encircling the weedy roundabout and the rotting inn sign. Mr. Tredgold locked the door of The Blue Moon behind him and handed the key to me.

"I wish you happiness of your new property," he said, and I saw him exchange what was almost a wink with James. Then he went over to his car, opened the door, and extracted a notice that read CLOSED UNTIL FURTHER NOTICE, which he hung on the front door. "Unnecessary, really," he said, "but one has to preserve the formalities."

After quite a lot more handshaking and promises of appointments to sign legal documents, Mr. Tredgold turned and walked toward his car. As he did so he said, almost to himself, "Poor old Captain Seb. I did my best. I did my best." Then he got into the car and drove off.

As James and I climbed into the Escort, it began to rain again. James raised the roof and windows and said, "And now for the infamous Golden Goose and the frozen pizza. Not to mention a drink. My God, what a dump. Poor Susan. Not much of an inheritance."

"No, it's not, is it?"

"It's a positive liability. There'll be property taxes to pay, and—"

I interrupted him. "What do you think Tredgold meant about stories of murders and ghosts and so on?"

"Heaven knows, but we'll soon be in a position to find out. Mr. Pargeter of The Golden Goose is supposed to have started them."

"Let's ask him," I said.

It was very pleasant to be back in the warm, dry, civilized

bar of The Golden Goose, eating inferior but hot pizza and drinking white wine (me) and tomato juice (James). As earlier, there were very few people in the pub, and it was easy to persuade Mr. Pargeter to sit down at our table and have a drink with us. I brought up the question of the murders and the haunting.

"Oh, that," said Pargeter, taking a swig of his beer. "For a start, not murders, but murder—just one. The haunting story started sometime later—pure imagination, of course. No, some years ago talk went round the village that Mr. Gardiner, the owner, had murdered his wife there. Pushed her in the river, or some such nonsense. He bought the place for her as a sort of hobby, and she ran it for a bit, and then went and got drowned in the river. Everyone thought Mr. Gardiner would sell after that, but he simply went on renting it out.

"Of course, we weren't open in those days, so there was no competition and the old Blue Moon did quite well. But you know how folks talk. One thing leads to another. Some chaps swore they saw a white lady walking down to the river from the pub. Drunk more than like, if you ask me. Anyhow, it didn't do The Blue Moon any good. And by that time we were open, and serving fine drinks and good food at fair prices, though I say it myself. So where did the custom come? You ask yourself." Mr. Pargeter laughed.

The sun came out again in its usual fitful April way as we left The Golden Goose, but we decided to keep the roof of the car up, just the same. After driving for some time in silence, James said, "I really am sorry, Susan."

"Why should you be sorry?"

"Well—it must be disappointing for you. A dump like that. Look, if it would be any help, I'll put it on the books of the same agents who are handling the Holland Park house. They're absolutely the best in London, and if anyone can get a halfway decent price for you, they can. I wouldn't advise local agents, because they'd know too much about the place." He took his eyes off the road for a split second and smiled at me. "If only there was a bridge over that damned river, the main London road runs close to the other side of it. The new tenant might pick up some passing trade that way. As it is, the only hope seems to be to sell it as a country cottage to some well-heeled Londoner." He paused, then said, "In fact, I'll tell you what. To save the agent's commission, I'll buy it off you myself and flog it to one of my clients. How's that?"

"James," I said, "you're being tremendously kind, but—"

He laughed. "Cousins must stick together. Don't give it a thought. When we get back to town, I'll drop you off at your place to change, and then we'll go out and have a bloody good dinner somewhere, and try to—"

"James," I said again. "Please listen to me for a moment. I don't intend to sell The Blue Moon."

"You *what*? My poor old ears must be going back on me."

"No, they're not. I intend to reopen The Blue Moon and run it myself—as a restaurant."

There was a small pause, full of incredulity. Then James said, "I simply don't know where to start. In the first place, it would have to be practically rebuilt. Where do you get the money?"

"I can manage it," I said. "I got a big insurance settlement when my parents were killed, and there's a good bit over from the sale of the Ealing house. Oh, I know The Blue Moon looks awful now, but there are some lovely things there. The bar and the brass footrail only need cleaning—well, the bar will have to be French polished, but that doesn't cost the earth. The kitchen is big and only needs some modern fittings and a water heater, and the room next to it will make a perfect dining room. I'll knock out the wall on the river side, and put in sliding glass doors and a shaded terrace—and when the weather is good, there'll be tables on the lawn running down to the water."

"All right," James said grudgingly. "I suppose it could be made quite attractive. But you know nothing about hotel management or cooking or—"

"As a matter of fact, I do."

"You do?"

"Yes. I told you I went to a finishing school in Switzerland. Actually, it was a very famous hotel school. I graduated from there, and since then I've been working up from the bottom at various hotels and restaurants in London. And if the bottom of the hotel business is not very amusing, it's extremely educational. I can run The Blue Moon on my head."

We drove on for a while in silence. Then suddenly James said, "I apologize, Susan. I misjudged you."

"That's all right," I said, and it was my turn to smile. "Is that dinner still on?"

"You bet it is."

CHAPTER

4

The months that followed were among the most exciting and most exhausting of my life. I scoured Danford and the surrounding villages for the best carpenters, builders, and electricians. Mr. Matthews, who had "kept an eye on the place" for Mr. Tredgold, proved a tower of strength, and I hired him as a general handyman and gardener. Of course there was a tremendous amount to be done, but little by little The Blue Moon began to take shape. The lovely old fixtures came to life, gleaming and glinting in the early summer sun. Inside and out, fresh paint lightened and brightened the old house. The lawn running down to the river was not exactly velvety—that would take years of work—but under Mr. Matthews's ministrations it became smooth and green. I deliberately left the woodlands on either side of it in their wild state, both for privacy and beauty, but we planted out the flower beds around the house, and also made a vegetable garden, because I was determined to serve home-grown food whenever I could.

I saw quite a lot of James during this period. As soon as The

Blue Moon was habitable, I sold the Kingston apartment and moved in, but I had to go to London frequently to choose furnishings and fabrics and to recruit my staff, and we nearly always lunched together.

One day he had exciting news. He had sold Uncle Sebastian's house for a very substantial price. Typically, his first thought was to offer me some of the money to help restore The Blue Moon, but I was able to assure him that I was managing all right. Nevertheless, it was a comforting feeling that there was financial backing there if I needed it.

Several times, on weekends, James drove down to Danford to inspect progress, and I could see that he was impressed. Certainly it was a very different place from the dismal, decaying wreck we had first seen that early April afternoon.

I was lucky to find a really first-class chef—a young man called Danny, who had graduated the year after I did from the same hotel school, taken the Cordon Bleu course in Paris, and also had clever but unfussy ideas of his own. He had been working as *sous-chef* in a big London hotel, which he hated, and he jumped at the idea of a smaller kitchen where he would be in complete charge. He brought with him a couple of kitchen boys, Pierre and Mike, whom he had trained himself. A girl, Daphne Wittering, who had been in my class at Lausanne, came as receptionist-housekeeper, and I managed to snaffle the headwaiter from a country house hotel, where he had just had a flaming row with the owner. The rest of the small staff, apart from the waiters, were local people—young, enthusiastic, and eager to learn.

The only person who tried to put a damper on everything was the unpleasant Mr. Pargeter from The Golden Goose. I suppose it was only natural, but I really didn't intend to interfere with his trade. I was after people who wanted excellent food, not frozen pizzas and tuna sandwiches, and I reckoned that he would still get the villagers in his bar. Nevertheless, he delighted in spreading predictions of gloom and doom, and was extremely rude to me on the rare occasions when we met.

At last, all was ready for the grand opening. James was very helpful with suggestions for discreet advertising, both locally and in some of the top-class London magazines. We put up big signs both in Danford village and at the head of the lane, crossed our fingers, and sat back to wait for our first customers. (Naturally James came to the opening evening, bringing with him a party of friends from London who could be relied on to spread the news, good or bad, by word of mouth.)

The rest, I think, is history. That is, The Blue Moon was a huge success. Food correspondents from London papers and magazines began coming along, scattering stars like fireworks over their columns. It seemed as if my dream had come true at last. Which was why it was so particularly awful when it happened.

It was a Wednesday evening in early October, about three months after we opened. We were booked up as usual for dinner—it was a cool, crisp day, pleasant for a drive to the country. Danny had put together a small but excellent menu, but every evening he had a "special"—an entrée featuring, if possible, fresh produce from the garden or fish from the river, or local game in season. October isn't an easy month for specials—in the good old days, we could have got native Colchester oysters, but pollution had just about put a stop to that. I remember that we'd had a talk—conference would have been too grand a word for it—in the morning: Danny, Pierre, Mike, Daphne, the headwaiter (who called himself Fernando, but was actually Fred), and myself.

I simply can't remember now who first suggested that there was a crop of big wild mushrooms ("horse mushrooms," my parents used to call them) growing in a meadow farther along the riverbank. I'm sure you know the sort I mean—big and flat and very black underneath, and with twice the flavor of your miserable little curled-up white cultivated ones. Anyhow, Danny was delighted, and soon the kitchen was full of them, and Danny had concocted a dish involving slivers of mushroom with veal medallions, brandy, all sorts of herbs and spices, and angel-hair noodles.

It was a very popular special. I remember several people remarking on it—old Sir Quinton and Lady Ponsonby, who had driven all the way down from Suffolk, and several people from London whom I didn't know. I was very busy that evening, so I didn't really have much time to notice the couple sitting in the corner near the kitchen door. (Well, somebody has to have that table, and they had booked very late.)

As always, however, I passed by the table to inquire if all was well. The woman was late middle-aged, somewhat flamboyantly dressed. She had ordered Danny's melon fan with orange sauce as a starter, and she waved her fork about as she speared the melon slices and declared the dish to be delicious. Her companion was a timid-looking young man in an open-neck shirt and slacks, who was sipping lobster bisque in a faintly apologetic manner. There seemed to be no problem there, so I went on to greet some newly arrived guests.

The first I knew of anything wrong was a horrified gasp from Fred—sorry, Fernando. I swung round to see him bending over the flamboyant lady, who had apparently collapsed with her head in her plate. In front of her was the evening's special dish, and from the fork in her hand it was clear that she had just taken a mouthful of it. The young man was sitting in frozen horror in front of a large steak.

Oh, God, I thought. *Not another drunk.* We'd had a few already.

It's extraordinary what people don't notice in a crowded dining room. Fernando and one of the waiters were able to get her into the kitchen, followed by her dining companion, before

33

more than a handful of people had cottoned on to the fact that anything was wrong; and even they didn't seem to be taking much notice.

We laid her on the floor on a bed of coats and towels, while the young man knelt beside her, whispering "Auntie Flora! Auntie Flora!" in a barely audible voice. I took a good look at the woman and suddenly realized that she wasn't drunk at all. I rushed to telephone the doctor.

Dr. Trumper was at his own dinner, but he came with commendable speed, making his way in by the back door, as I had suggested. It took only a minute or two to establish that the poor lady was dead. The doctor stood up and looked at me very gravely. "Miss Gardiner," he said, "I'm afraid this is a matter for the police."

A cold hand closed over my heart. "What do you mean?"

"This lady has every appearance of having been poisoned. I'll call Inspector Darlington at once, but meanwhile I'm afraid you'll have to ask all your guests not to leave. Has anyone gone since this incident happened?"

Daphne, who sat at the desk between the bar and the dining room, confirmed that nobody had left the restaurant. In view of the weather, the big French windows leading to the lawn were securely closed, and Danny assured us that the kitchen door had opened only to admit Dr. Trumper. With a sinking heart, I made my way back into the dining room and clinked a fork on a glass for silence. When it had been achieved, I said, "Ladies and gentlemen, I'm afraid there has been an accident. This won't take long, but I have to ask none of you to leave until . . ." Until when? Until what? I honestly didn't know. I skated round the problem. "It'll just be a question of giving your names and addresses. A pure formality."

A very ancient lady, who clearly remembered such things from her youth, squealed, "A raid! A police raid! Oh, how devastatingly exciting!"

'Not a raid at all, madam," I said, trying hard to keep a smile in my voice. "It will only take a few minutes. Meanwhile, to compensate for any inconvenience, The Blue Moon will be happy to serve drinks on the house to anybody who would like them." This produced a round of applause and a little laughter. "Now, please do get on with your dinners and enjoy them." I had already told the waiters to inform any diner who tried to order it that the special was no longer available; but this was unnecessary. Poor Miss Fotheringay—we had discovered her name from her distraught nephew—had had the last portion.

Then, trying to look as if there was absolutely nothing unusual about a suspected poisoning at a first-class restaurant, I made my way back into the kitchen and virtually into the arms of Detective Inspector Darlington of the Danford police.

I didn't really know Inspector Darlington at all—my only dealings with the local police had been with the uniformed branch over transferring liquor licenses and arranging for parking and so on—but I had met Darlington—in a place like Danford, everybody knows everybody else—and I practically threw my arms round his neck.

"Inspector, please, please! Let my people go!"

"I say, I say, no need to get biblical, Miss Gardiner." Darlington smiled. "Now, let's get this straight. As I understand it, Miss Fotheringay and her nephew, Mr. Brandon—" He nodded toward the young man, who had collapsed onto a kitchen stool and was being revived by Pierre with a glass of rather good brandy "—were occupying a table near the door to the kitchen. I gather nothing has been touched there."

"Nothing except that we brought the poor lady out here—"

"I understand, Miss Gardiner. Now, Miss Fotheringay had ordered a veal and mushroom special—the last remaining portion—which was prepared in the kitchen and brought to her by Montague, the waiter." Montague, white-faced, nodded agreement "Nobody else in the dining room could have tampered with it. Nobody could have come into the kitchen and—"

"I should bloody well say not!" Danny was outraged.

"Then this is what I'll do," Darlington said comfortingly. "I'll station a constable at the dining-room door, and have him take the names and addresses and check identity where possible of each guest as he or she leaves. I can't see that any more is necessary. So you can go back and tell your guests so."

"Oh, thank you, Inspector!" I was nearly in tears.

"Any more to come? People who've booked and not turned up yet?" Darlington asked.

I shook my head. "We were fully booked, and in any case we don't accept reservations after nine o'clock."

"Then that's that, Miss Gardiner. Leave everything else to us."

Back in the dining room, the atmosphere was almost convivial. I don't think any of the other diners really believed that anything more than an accident had happened, and most of them were taking full advantage of the free drinks. The fact that I had to tell them that no more food could be served was received with a few disgruntled murmurs, but the promise of free ice cream (not to mention drinks) from the bar seemed to mollify the grumblers.

Before long, people started to leave, and the constable at the door reported no objections to imparting names and addresses, backed up where possible by credit cards and drivers' licenses. So the public went home and left The Blue Moon to cope with its own nightmare. As I said a polite "Good night" to my last departing guest and headed for the kitchen, I was conscious of one overriding feeling: I wished with all my heart and soul that James was there. I think this was the first moment when I admitted to myself how dependent on him I had become, and it gave me a vaguely resentful feeling.

I suppose I had never quite come to terms with the trauma

of losing my entire family in one shocking incident. I had concentrated on coping with life alone, toughing it out, and I thought I had made a pretty good job of it. And then, out of the blue, James had come along, and suddenly I wasn't without a family after all. So I had instinctively turned to him for the support I didn't think I needed anymore. Damn him.

CHAPTER

5

To tell you the truth, I haven't any very clear recollection of the next few hours. The place seemed to be swarming with policemen and doctors and photographers and fingerprint experts, and all the other paraphernalia of a murder investigation—because, as Inspector Darlington explained in his slow, comfortable East Anglian voice, although the whole thing might turn out to have been an accident, this was the moment to pick up on clues, while the trail was hot.

Poor Miss Fotheringay was removed in an ambulance to the local hospital, where a postmortem examination was to be performed immediately. Her nephew, whose full name turned out to be Nigel Fotheringay Brandon, was interviewed at great length by Darlington, and eventually allowed to go home—or, to be exact, to his aunt's home, Anderton House, in Much Matchingly, a village some fifteen miles away.

I realized then that I should have known who Miss Fotheringay was. I had never met her, but I knew of her as a rich spinster who lived in a very splendid manor house, and had been one of the people who had signed a petition against the permit to allow reconstruction and development of The Blue Moon, claiming that it would spoil the amenities of the neighborhood. There was a grim sort of irony in the fact that the first time she had got over her chagrin and come to dine with us, this tragedy should have happened.

Next, of course, came exhaustive interviews with Danny, the kitchen staff, and the waiters—the only people with access to the kitchen.

I could have saved Inspector Darlington and his faithful Sergeant a lot of trouble by telling them exactly how our system worked—but of course they had to find out everything firsthand. Briefly, while Danny was in undisputed charge of the kitchen, various culinary duties were relegated. Pierre was already turning into an excellent sauce chef, which was his exclusive domain; Mike was in charge of the actual cooking of the vegetables and was also what the French call *chef du partie*, meaning the person who puts everything together, including hors d'oeuvres and buffets, and makes them look marvelous.

The routine part of vegetable preparation—peeling potatoes, slicing, and so forth—was carried out under Mike's watchful eye by three village girls, Annie, Mary, and Doris; but none of them had been allowed to touch any of the ingredients for the special, except for peeling the shallots and carrots and reducing them to shreds in a food processor. Danny cooked all the meat himself, added Pierre's sauces as required, and left Mike to assemble the whole into an appetizing dish Apart from two dishwashers, that completed the actual kitchen staff. Eight people.

Fernando, the headwaiter, never went into the kitchen at all. He was in charge of seating, of course, and of the wine. We had a good cellar, in every sense—that is, the building was equipped with a most adequate underground storage room that was much larger than we needed for the two beer barrels (I had kept the blue and white porcelain handles, you may be sure), and left plenty of room for wine to be stored at a suitable temperature.

James had been invaluable in helping me to select a small and very drinkable yet not outrageously expensive wine list. In the dining room itself, we had a rack of red wines at room temperature and a small refrigerator for keeping a selection of our most popular white wines that could be drunk cold immediately.

The dining room was not enormous, so we employed only three waiters, one of whom was always off duty. They were an assorted lot—a charming Iraqi called Ali who was escaping political persecution in his own country (I often wondered if Ali was really his name—*all* Arabs can't be called Ali); a young English boy, Steve, fresh from hotel school, who was useful because he had had a rather sketchy but formal training; and a somewhat shiftless character in his thirties, Montague, who had answered an advertisement I had put in one of the hotel-oriented magazines. He claimed to have experience, but I doubted it. Frankly, I thought he was the kind of drifter who likes to think of himself as a soldier of fortune, and I rather hoped that he would find some suitable elderly lady and drift out of my life. To do him justice, he was very good-looking.

It was Montague who had served Miss Fotheringay's table. I might have known it. He had taken her order and that of her nephew, and gone into the kitchen to relay them to Danny and his team. Nigel Brandon's steak was, of course, selected and freshly grilled by Danny, while Miss Fotheringay's veal-and-mushroom special was assembled by Mike and Pierre, and put on a tray for Montague to serve. I had to admit to myself that Pierre, Mike, and Montague all had the chance to tamper with it. Nobody else, as far as I could see.

It was around midnight when Inspector Darlington was called to the telephone. We were all utterly exhausted—with the exception of Darlington and his men, who seemed as fresh as daisies. He was very terse on the phone, confining his conversation to sharply spoken monosyllables—"Yes," "I see," "When?"—while scribbling busily in his notebook. When he rang off, he came over to me, his face very grave.

I sighed, more from tiredness than anything else.

"Bad news, Inspector?"

"I'm afraid so, Miss Gardiner. That was the pathologist on the line. I'm afraid the poor lady was definitely poisoned." He smiled grimly. "The doctor said we had been lucky."

"Lucky? What on earth do you mean?"

"Well, the poison was amanitine, together with phalloidine. That can only come from the *Amanita phalloides*."

"Oh, please talk English."

"Very well. It's the Death Cap mushroom, also known as Destroying Angel. And the laboratory has found traces of it in the remains of Miss Fotheringay's veal dish that we sent for analysis."

"Oh, my God! But it can't have been—I mean, that dish was very popular. Lots of people had it and were perfectly all right. In fact, Miss Fotheringay had the very last portion."

"Unfortunately, that's correct." The Inspector half smiled. "Your kitchen system is very efficient, Miss Gardiner. As soon as the last portion was served, all the cooking pots and containers were thoroughly washed up and put away. So we have no way of telling how many other people may be affected."

"But, Inspector, I just told you—"

"That's why the doctor said we were lucky. It seems that Miss Fotheringay had an untypically quick reaction to the poison, probably due to the fact that she was suffering from an incipient stomach ulcer. Normally, the symptoms take some hours to appear—normally six or seven, but it can be up to fifteen."

I felt sick. I said, "Well, we've got the names and addresses of the people who were here at the time. Or rather, you have."

"Yes, Miss Gardiner, and I shall have to telephone them all. But there must have been people who had already left the restaurant before the incident—"

"Incident!" I wanted to shout, but it came out as a mutter, and the Inspector continued unperturbed.

"You, of course, have the names of all the people who booked tables, and we shall have to try to contact all of them, and tell them to go to the nearest hospital at once. All who ate the special dish, that is."

I nodded. "What's the cure?"

"I'm afraid there isn't one. No known antidote, that is. They'll all have to have lavage—that's washing out the stomach—and/or induced vomiting."

"You realize this'll be the end of my restaurant, don't you, Inspector?"

Darlington looked at me curiously. "Your priorities seem a little strange, Miss Gardiner. I'm trying to save lives. This poison is over ninety percent fatal."

"Of course. I'm sorry." I stood up. "You start your telephoning, and I'll find my booking list."

It took just about the rest of the night, but in the end we contacted everybody who had eaten the special dish. The reactions were mixed, to say the least. Nobody wants to be woken up in the middle of the night and told to go to hospital and have his stomach washed out. Poor Danny just sat in the kitchen and sobbed. Everybody else fell asleep, and the police finally went home.

In the morning, Inspector Darlington drove up, infuriatingly chirpy, in his police car.

"What's the news?" I hardly dared to ask.

Darlington beamed. "Good," he said. "No trace of poison in any of your other guests."

"Thank God for that."

"But you do realize what this means, Miss Gardiner?"

"It means that we've only succeeded in killing one customer," I said, trying to force a smile.

"It means more than that, I'm afraid. It means that Miss Fotheringay's dish was deliberately tampered with. It means murder."

Trying to sound as unhysterical as I could, I said, "Well, thank goodness it'll be you in charge of the investigation, Inspector, and not a stranger."

His face darkened, and I knew at once that I had said the wrong thing. "I'm afraid not, Miss Gardiner."

"But whyever not? You're—"

"I'm not senior enough, for one thing, miss. Nobody under Detective Chief Superintendent can handle a murder these days. And in any case, the Chief Constable has called in the Yard."

"Scotland Yard!" I was horrified.

"Yes, miss," said Darlington, full of gloom. "The Chief Superintendent will be along this afternoon."

And that was how I came to meet Chief Superintendent Henry Tibbett.

CHAPTER

It was decided from the beginning that the team from Scotland Yard would stay at The Blue Moon. Of the four bedrooms, one had been turned into a bathroom, which adjoined the one I occupied. The other two, plus the second bathroom, formed a suite in which I could accommodate friends. I also let it out on rare occasions to visitors who came from so far afield that it was impossible—as well as dangerous, considering the amount of wine they consumed—for them to drive home. The Chief Superintendent was to have the big double bedroom and the Inspector the smaller single one.

Frankly, I didn't know what to expect when the sleek black police car drew up in the driveway that afternoon. I was surprised at first that there were three people in it, rather than only two—but then I realized that the third must be the driver. My next thought was, for an avowed feminist, shaming. For sitting next to the driver was a woman—middle age with black curly hair streaked with gray, a peaches-and-cream complexion, and a ready smile. It simply hadn't occurred to me that Inspector Reynolds might be a woman—and yet, why not, for heaven's sake? The question was—where was she going to sleep?

In the back of the car, the Chief Superintendent looked reassuring—tall, dark, and brawny, and good-looking in a rugged sort of way. The driver I hardly noticed—a smallish man with graying sandy hair and blue eyes.

I hurried out to greet them as the Chief Superintendent got out of the back of the car—and then I stopped dead in amazement. Because the dark man I had presumed to be the Chief Superintendent was opening the driver's door for him and saying "Well, here we are, sir."

The driver got out and went round to open the door for my postulated lady Inspector, whom he took by the arm and brought up to meet me.

"You must be Miss Susan Gardiner," he said. "May I introduce myself? I'm Henry Tibbett, and this is my wife, Emmy."

I shook hands in a sort of daze. "And this," Tibbett went on, indicating the dark man, "is Inspector Derek Reynolds."

"How do you do?" I said feebly.

Henry Tibbett smiled almost shyly. "I hope you don't mind my bringing Emmy along. She has nothing to do with the investigation, of course, but we have some good friends at Cregwell, not too far away. The Manciples."

"I don't think I know them," I said. "I'm pretty much a stranger in these parts myself."

The Tibbetts exchanged an amused glance, and Emmy said, "You soon will. They're quite a remarkable family."

"If accommodation is a problem," Henry went on, "Emmy can always stay at Cregwell Grange. She's planning to hire a car anyway, and Cregwell is only just over the border in Fenshire."

"No, no, that's perfectly all right, Chief Superintendent. There are two beds in the main guest room."

"Splendid. How kind of you, Miss Gardiner. Now, let's get our luggage in, and we can begin."

Inspector Darlington was along just five minutes after Tibbett telephoned him, and the two men, together with Reynolds, closeted themselves in the deserted bar, while I helped Mrs. Tibbett ("Please call me Emmy—everybody does.") to get the bags out of the car and upstairs, and arranged for her to hire a self-drive Mini. As soon as it arrived, she set off to visit her friends in Cregwell.

Meanwhile, I offered the three detectives the use of my office for greater privacy, and they adjourned there, while I waited nervously in the bar, along with Hilda, the barmaid. Hilda was a local girl, buxom, cheeky, and attractive, and she seemed to be the only one of us who was quite unaffected by the murder.

"Ooh, wot an 'orrible thing to 'appen," she said cheerfully as she rearranged bottles and polished glasses; but she might have been talking about an electricity outage or the illness of a friend's dog.

I didn't have to worry about the evening meal, because the police had closed the kitchen for the day while they took everything apart and sent various foodstuffs away for laboratory testing. Daphne had spent the morning contacting people with reservations to put them off. I had a strong suspicion that I wouldn't have to worry much about the kitchen in the future either. Who was going to come and eat in a restaurant that served poisoned food?

After what seemed an eternity, Inspector Reynolds emerged from the office and asked if I would mind stepping in. I stepped.

Henry Tibbett greeted me with a reassuring grin and invited me to sit down. He started off right away.

"Well, Miss Gardiner, there doesn't seem to be any mystery about what happened. Somehow, pieces of that mushroom with the unpronounceable name that is known as the Destroying Angel were introduced into Miss Fotheringay's dish. The fact that nobody else who ate the special was affected makes it clear that it was intended for her. Now, first question. Does the Destroying Angel grow in the woods around here?"

I swallowed hard. I'd have given a lot to twist the truth, but I didn't feel I could—and anyway I felt sure that those deep blue eyes wouldn't be fooled.

"Yes," I said. "I believe it does."

"What makes you believe that?" Tibbett's voice was very gentle.

"I . . . well, when I first came here, I was warned about it by Mr. Matthews, my gardener. It looks so pretty, you see—white and graceful—and people, especially children, are attracted by it, and might eat it. Of course, nobody local would dream of—"

Tibbett nodded, with a glance at Darlington. "So the Inspector tells me. I congratulate you on the accuracy of your answer."

This nettled me. "I am an accurate person, Chief Superintendent."

"Let's drop the 'Chief Superintendent,' or we'll be here all night. Mr. Tibbett will do very well. Or, better still, Henry."

"Thank you," I said, and I hoped I sounded icy.

"So the fungus could have been gathered by an unsuspecting stranger—or a murderous local."

"I suppose so." I didn't at all like the line things were taking.

"An unsuspecting stranger," Tibbett went on, "might possibly have eaten the stuff himself. But he would hardly have put it deliberately into the food of one of your guests."

I said, "Do let's stop beating about the bush, Mr. Tibbett. The only people who had access to that plate were Pierre and Mike, the chef's assistants—neither of whom is local, although they've lived here for a few months. Oh, and Montague, the waiter—but he's not local either. I shouldn't think he knows a puffball from a pouffe. In any case, why should anybody want to kill Miss Fotheringay?"

"Now we're getting closer to it," I heard Darlington grunt into his pipe.

Tibbett said, "Which brings us to the question of motive."

"Which brings us to Mr. Nigel Fotheringay Brandon," remarked Inspector Reynolds, making his first contribution to the conversation.

"Exactly," said Tibbett. "It does look as if he is the obvious suspect. At the moment, that is. Miss Fotheringay was a very rich woman, as you probably know, and Mr. Brandon is her only nephew. Unless she left an extremely eccentric will, he probably inherits everything. No wonder he was upset last night."

"Appeared to be upset," muttered Darlington.

"Is Brandon a local man?" This from Tibbett.

Darlington answered at once. "No, of course not. Lives in London, but comes down to spend occasional weekends with his aunt Flora. Weekends, you notice. Not midweek. And yet he was here on Wednesday evening. We've got his address, naturally—somewhere in the docklands. Bedsitter."

"Not very wealthy, then." It was not a question but a statement, on a note of triumph, from Reynolds.

Tibbett turned to me. "Miss Gardiner, is there any chance that Mr. Brandon might know that the Destroying Angel fungus grows around here, and where to find it?"

I shrugged. "How can I possibly know? All I can say is that if he did, he must have done some local research."

"If you ask me," said Inspector Reynolds, although nobody had asked him anything, "he bribed some local person to get the stuff for him and then he mixed it into his aunt's food."

Henry Tibbett's sandy eyebrows went up, and he looked at me. "Any comments, Miss Gardiner?"

"Plenty," I said grimly. "First of all, if she'd been fed the poison in her own home, and he was her heir and her only visitor at the time, he'd have been arrested right away. So he had to bring her out to a restaurant—*my* restaurant—to give it to her. O.K., that makes sense. But how on earth did he get it on to her plate, for God's sake? She never left the table. He was having steak, plain and simple, and you don't just say 'Here, Auntie, try a mouthful of my delicious steak'—and give a fork-ful with white mushrooms hanging all over it. It's just not on. If he's a murderer, he's also the biggest fool I've ever come across."

Henry Tibbett nodded approvingly, but Darlington broke in. "You're forgetting something," he said. "As we know, normally this is a slow-acting poison, and shows no symptoms for five or six hours, or even more. He had no way of knowing that someone in her medical condition would react immediately."

Reynolds said, "On the contrary, he was probably the only person who did know. Apart from her doctor, that is."

"Dr. Trumper?" I laughed. "Don't be silly. He was nowhere near The Blue Moon last night. We had to interrupt him at his dinner at home to come and examine the poor lady."

Reynolds smiled—a rather nasty, superior smile, I thought. He said, "Dr. Trumper wasn't Miss Fotheringay's doctor, Miss Gardiner. Brandon told Inspector Darlington that she went to a very upstage character in Harley Street, as you might expect." He paused. "Have you got that list, Darlington?"

Inspector Darlington opened his briefcase and brought out a couple of sheets of paper. To me, in an apologetic voice, he said, "This is the list of names and addresses of the people who dined here last night, Miss Gardiner."

Reynolds took the list and scanned it, running his eye down

the columns. Then he said, "Ah, here we are. Dr. and Mrs. Herbert Chomondly, of Harley Street, London."

"Chumley," I said, without thinking. Of course, that's the way the name should be pronounced in English. I looked up and saw a twinkle in Henry Tibbett's blue eyes. He wasn't missing a thing.

Reynolds glared, and went on. "Inspector Darlington telephoned this list through to me this morning, and I called Dr. Chom—Dr. Chumley. His secretary confirmed that Miss Fotheringay was one of his patients. And he and his wife dined here last night. Neither of them had the mushroom dish, but they were here."

"Oh, don't be silly," I said. "That's nothing but a coincidence. Dr. and Mrs. Chomondly are regular customers—they have a weekend cottage near here, and they quite often drive down from London during the week for dinner. Are you seriously suggesting that one guest could tamper with another guest's food? And in any case, I remember now, the doctor and his wife dined early and had already left when . . . when it happened. Quite apart from anything else, what could a famous doctor have to gain by the death of a wealthy patient?"

Henry Tibbett said slowly, "I'm inclined to agree with Miss Gardiner. But Miss Fotheringay's will hasn't been read yet. We're in touch with her solicitors, and we'll soon know what's in it. Of course, Nigel Brandon is the obvious beneficiary, but elderly ladies do sometimes leave large legacies to their doctors—not to mention cats' homes and so on. We'll keep an eye on Dr. Chomondly." He pronounced it correctly, of course. "However, the first thing is to talk to your staff. They're all here?"

"All here, and all going crazy, with the kitchen shut and nothing to do."

Tibbett grinned. "We'll try to make things a bit more lively

50

for them. Let's start with the chef. Danny . . ." He consulted his notebook. "Danny Allbright, isn't it?"

"I suppose so." I grinned back. "We never think of him as anything but Danny."

Of course, I don't know exactly what happened at those interviews, but I got secondhand reports from everybody at almost intolerable length. Who knew about the Destroying Angel and where it was to be found? Who actually handled Miss Fotheringay's plate? All last night's questions all over again. What emerged clearly was that Tibbett had made a big hit with everybody, while Reynolds was "a bit stuck-up" and might even be a bully. I found myself agreeing. Anyhow, it seemed that the whole staff had volunteered to prepare dinner for the Scotland Yard team (including Mrs. Tibbett, when she returned) once the police had finished with the kitchen.

Meanwhile, as far as I was concerned, a far more important thing had happened. I was trying to rest upstairs when I heard a murmur of tires in the drive. I rushed to the window, but I knew already that it could only be the white Ford Escort. I don't remember my feet touching the stairs as I flew down them, and the next moment I was clinging to James like a shipwreck survivor to a floating plank.

"My poor darling Susan." He stroked my hair gently. "I was in Paris, and I only just heard. I came right away."

I tried to remember that I resented being so reliant on this man, but it didn't seem to work. I almost never cry, but it took all my self-control to say, calmly, "It was sweet of you to come, James. Come in and have a drink, and I'll tell you all about it."

James was, as I might have expected, practical as well as comforting. "I've heard of Henry Tibbett," he said. "He's supposed to be good. Leave it to him—he'll get an arrest, whether it turns out to be the nephew or the doctor or even, heaven forbid, one of the staff. The important thing is to keep the reputation of The Blue Moon out of this, and I'm sure he'll be able to do that."

"But nobody will want to come and eat at a restaurant that serves poison!"

"You'd be surprised. A little notoriety can be very useful. Haven't you ever heard that there's no such thing as bad publicity?" James laughed. "Come on, Susan. Cheer up. Let's go out and get a meal somewhere. I presume the police have closed you up for the day."

"Yes and no," I said. "That is, we're closed to the public— you must have seen the notice—but the staff are making a sort of family dinner later on for the Scotland Yard men and myself. Oh, and Mrs. Tibbett."

"Mrs. Tibbett? I didn't know senior C.I.D. men took their wives along with them on cases."

"They don't," I explained, "but Emmy has friends only a few miles away in Fenshire, and she's hired a car of her own, and I can put them both up. She and Henry—"

"Christian names already, is it?" James sounded amused but also just a little put out.

"Well," I said, "he's not exactly your run-of-the-mill policeman. You'll see. You're invited to dinner, naturally, if you're brave enough."

"Idiot girl," said James, and kissed me lightly on the forehead, which gave me a ridiculous amount of pleasure.

We found Henry Tibbett and Derek Reynolds in the bar, their interviews concluded, drinking a half pint of bitter each. There was nobody behind the bar—Hilda must either have been sent home or asked to leave them in peace—and their heads were together in earnest discussion over their open notebooks. Any conspiratorial air, however, disappeared as soon as James and I came in.

"Ah, there you are, Miss Gardiner," said Henry. He gave James a slightly quizzical look, and I said quickly, "This is my cousin, James Gardiner. He was in Paris when . . . when it happened, and he's been kind enough to come and give me moral support."

"Delighted to meet you, Mr. Gardiner. I'm Henry Tibbett and this is Inspector Derek Reynolds." Hands were politely shaken, and then Henry said, "James Gardiner? Of Blumfield, Lebrune and Whittaker?"

James looked surprised but nodded. Henry said to me, "Your cousin is a well-known young man, Miss Gardiner. In business circles, that is. Maybe you don't read the financial sections of the newspapers."

"Not much," I admitted. I felt a bit depressed. For some reason I didn't fancy James being a celebrity.

As if reading my thoughts, Henry said, "One of the up-and-coming young men, so they say."

"Thank you, sir," said James.

It was at that moment that the bar door flew open, and Emmy Tibbett came in like a small, plump whirlwind.

"Oh, Henry, I've had the most marvelous time at Cregwell! The Bishop—" She broke off as she realized that the bar was not empty. "Oh, I'm so sorry. I'm Emmy Tibbett."

Once again, introductions were made all round, and then I suggested a drink. "I presume our redoubtable Hilda has gone home, so please let me serve you. On the house, or what's left of it."

I slipped behind the bar and began taking orders.

James said, "Susan is being unduly pessimistic, Chief Superintendent. She seems to think that this poisoning will ruin her business. Personally, I think it will be the making of it. Provided," he added dryly, "that an arrest is made soon and shows that the restaurant was in no way involved."

Henry grinned. "I suppose you young men in the City are accustomed to demanding fast results and getting them," he said. "With us it takes a little longer. People's whole futures are at stake, and even their lives—not, thank God, by hanging any longer, but if we arrest the wrong person and leave a murderer at large, he or she may decide to do it again."

"Sir," Reynolds said in his pompous way, "Nigel Brandon isn't going to murder anybody else. He's just after his aunt's money."

Henry looked at him reprovingly, in a walls-have-ears manner, and said, "Well, it's far too soon yet to come to any conclusion. We haven't even spoken to anybody outside The Blue Moon. Now, Emmy, tell us about the Manciples and what the Bishop has been up to."

Emmy needed no encouragement. It seemed that the Manciples were an obviously loony Irish family who lived at Cregwell Grange, the looniest of the lot being the retired Bishop of Bugolaland, who was eccentric to the point of idiocy and was a mastermind at crossword puzzles. Apparently his greeting to Emmy had been "Ah, Mrs. Tibbett. Why sport a mac in an English rainstorm? To be secretive, of course."

Since the day was sunny, and Emmy was wearing a tweed suit, she hadn't cottoned on to the fact that this was a crossword clue until the Bishop added cryptically, "Two words."

There was a lot of speculation around the bar, until Henry came up triumphantly with the answer. "In camera." I confess that the whole thing seemed baffling and stupid to me, but I have since been told that any aficionado of the more complicated kind of British crossword would have solved it in a trice.

Just then, the bar door was flung open again and Fred (alias Fernando) announced, with ceremony, "Ladies and gentlemen, dinner is served."

CHAPTER

7

Despite the circumstances, dinner was a remarkably cheerful meal. Montague had retired, near hysterical, to his lodgings after his interview with Scotland Yard, and it was Steve's evening off anyway, so we were waited on by Ali, whose English seemed to have deteriorated badly. Henry remarked that it had been difficult to interview him without an interpreter, and my eyebrows rose a mental notch, because he had never had any trouble in communicating with the guests. A good protection, it seemed to me, against awkward questions. (I should perhaps explain here that Ali should have been off duty the previous evening but was being paid overtime to work, as we were so full.)

In any case, Tibbett did reveal that Steve had apparently never even heard of the Destroying Angel, that Montague admitted that he had been warned against it (he could hardly deny that, because, as I belatedly remembered, I had administered the warning myself) but had never seen one, and that Ali didn't seem to know what a mushroom was, let alone *Amanita phalloides*.

As for the kitchen staff, they had heard of the deadly fungus but naturally denied having picked it. Pierre had done the actual gathering of the mushrooms for the special dish. He had nearly exploded in Gallic fury when it was suggested that he might have picked some of the Destroying Angel in error. "In France," he had said, "one understands such things." Adding that he had picked his mushrooms in a grassy meadow, while the Destroying Angel grows in woods.

We also heard some more Manciple stories from Emmy. Violet, the Major's wife and notoriously vague, had apparently decided to learn to drive at the age of fifty-five and, having somehow passed her test, had driven straight through the side door of the local grocery store, saying "But I always come in this way."

James was a good conversationalist, as always: Only Reynolds said little and concentrated on the food. I can't say I blame him. Danny had excelled himself, with a delicate watercress soup and delectable salmon cooked in puff pastry on a bed of fennel, followed by one of his apricot and almond tarts. This latter prompted Inspector Reynolds to make one of his rare remarks of the evening—"Almonds, eh? No cyanide, I trust!"—which fell very flat.

Fred served our best white Burgundy and had some himself (unheard-of on a normal evening), and allowed quite a spicing of Cockney to seep through his carefully assumed Italian accent. As I said, it was a good and enjoyable dinner, and yet I felt that Henry was on the alert all the time, watching everyone, hearing everything, and missing nothing. A good policeman, I decided, a good friend, and a dangerous enemy.

The next morning had been designated for the police to visit Miss Fotheringay's house and to interview Nigel Brandon, who had stayed there rather than going back to London, which made me doubt his frequent assertions on the evening of the murder that his frightfully important job made it imperative for him to get back.

I knew that Henry and Reynolds were planning to drive over to Anderton House to talk to the young man, and so it was a surprise when, in answer to a frantic ringing of the front doorbell, I found Brandon panting on my doorstep at nine o'clock. In contrast to the informality of his dinner attire, he was neatly dressed in a pin-striped suit with waistcoat complete, but his manner showed the same aggressive timidity as on the evening of his aunt's death.

"Scotland Yard! I have to see the man from Scotland Yard!"

"I thought he was coming to see you, Mr. Brandon," I said.

He waved a feebly excited arm. "London!" he cried, as if no further explanation was necessary. "Will!"

"I'm afraid I don't quite understand—"

"I think I do," said a voice behind me, and I turned to see Henry Tibbett in the hallway. "I've just had a call. Miss Fotheringay's solicitor is going to read her will in his London office at twelve o'clock today."

"That's right." Nigel Brandon sounded grateful. "So of course I must—"

"Of course," Henry said soothingly. "But there's plenty of time. Why don't you come in? May we use your office again, Miss Gardiner?"

"Anything you like."

'In fact," said Henry, "why don't you sit in with us, Miss Gardiner? Then you can corroborate Mr. Brandon's statements."

It seemed a bit odd to me, but I was beginning to realize that Tibbett was not exactly an ordinary policeman. So soon the three of us, plus the inevitable Reynolds, were installed in my office.

Grudgingly, Brandon admitted that he knew of the existence of a poisonous fungus known as the Destroying Angel and that he had heard it grew in the neighborhood.

"How did you know that, Mr. Brandon?"

"Oh, somebody told me." Again the ineffective wave of the arm. "Aunt Flora, I think."

Henry's eyebrows went up. "Miss Fotheringay? Was she an expert on fungi?"

"If you live in these parts," Brandon said with an unexpected show of spirit, "you don't have to be an expert to have heard of the Destroying Angel."

This was so true that I almost applauded. "Perfectly correct," I said. Reynolds made a note and scowled.

"But she didn't notice any in her dish?"

"Well, she couldn't, could she? Not after they'd been chopped up and covered in brown gravy and mixed with all the rest." Brandon's air of confidence seemed to rise all the time.

"Very well," said Henry. "Now, I understand you were served by Montague. Which of you was served first?"

"Aunt Flora, of course. At least they know the right way of doing things in this establishment."

"I understand your table was near the door to the kitchen?"

"Yes." Brandon shot me an unfriendly glance. "Far too near. All that coming and going."

I felt obliged to defend Fred. "You—or rather, your aunt—made your booking very late, you know. It was the only table available."

"Anyhow," Henry said pacifically, "Montague came out of the kitchen with both dishes on a tray—right?"

"Yes."

"And he served your aunt first, and then you?"

"I've already told you so."

"What about the wine? You did have wine?"

"Of course. A bottle of Burgundy. Fernando brought it just

58

about the same time as the food. He poured a little into my glass for me to sample."

"Even though your aunt was paying for the dinner?"

Nigel Brandon had the grace to blush slightly. "It was a courtesy."

"I see. And then what happened?"

"He filled our glasses and went away. We began to eat."

"Was anything said?"

"My aunt took a mouthful and remarked how very delicious her dish was," said Brandon, wrinkling his nose in disgust. "And then—it happened."

"Had you started your steak?"

"Just one mouthful."

"One more question, Mr. Brandon. Why were you staying at Anderton House?"

"I often stay there."

"Yes—at weekends. But this was a Wednesday."

Silence.

"Had you come down to discuss anything special? Like money, for example?"

"I consider that an impertinent question."

Henry smiled. "It is, of course. But this is a murder investigation, and I really must have an answer."

After an uneasy silence, Brandon said, "Well, actually, if you must know—yes. I had—have a chance to buy into a very lucrative company, but it means capital, which I don't have."

"And did your aunt agree to provide the money?"

There was a little pause before Brandon said, "She hadn't made up her mind."

Henry stood up. "Well," he said, glancing at his watch, "I think we should go now."

"We?"

"Inspector Reynolds and I will be at the reading of the will.

Can we give you a lift? We'll be coming back here afterward."

"Thank you," Brandon said icily. "I prefer to drive myself."

"As you wish," said Henry, with a friendly smile.

I found Emmy Tibbett and James together in the bar, having a beer and chatting amiably. James said, "Hi, Susan. Emmy is going to take me over to Cregwell to meet these marvelous Manciples. Coming?"

"You know perfectly well I'm far too busy." I was aware that I sounded snappy. "We're fully open today, you know. Light lunches, but dinner as usual—if we have any customers."

"Pity," said James. "It should be fun. Don't expect us back to lunch."

I told myself that it was ridiculous to be jealous of a plump, middle-age married woman—but there it was. I forced a smile.

"Have a lovely time," I said, and went off to discuss menus with Danny in the kitchen. On the way, Daphne told me that there had been five cancellations for dinner already. Just what I needed to cheer me up.

As James had predicted, he and Emmy did not appear for lunch. There were a few locals in the bar chewing over the gory details of the murder with Hilda. We sold two plowman's lunches—one to an uncouth commercial traveler who said he'd had to come to us because The Golden Goose was so full and he was in a hurry. Damn Mr. Pargeter.

Henry and Derek Reynolds were back before Emmy and James, even though they had stopped off at Anderton House, taken a look round, and come back with a sheaf of papers from Miss Fotheringay's desk. There had been no surprises about the Fotheringay will. Apart from a few small bequests to faithful servants and some pieces of jewelry left to old friends, the lot went to Nigel Brandon. A little matter of a couple of million, plus the house.

"Sounds like plenty of motive," I said.

"Sounds like!" said Derek Reynolds.

I was beginning to feel like either Rosencrantz or Guildenstern, hovering on the fringes of the real story, implicated and yet in utter ignorance. I hoped that Shakespeare's final throwaway remark that they were dead would not apply to me too. Meanwhile, a bland and creamy chicken special had been arranged, with not a mushroom in sight. So far, we had ten uncanceled dinners out of an original fifty. I hadn't even bothered to open the morning newspaper, but I did so now. Of course, The Blue Moon was all over the front pages. Daphne had been doing a splendid job keeping the press at bay, but they'd been battering on the closed doors the day before, and nobody could stop them photographing the outside of the building. Fortunately for us, it seemed that they were getting any information they could from Darlington and his men.

With The Blue Moon fully functioning, at least in theory, I couldn't really manage without my office, so I opened up a small, little-used room known as the snug bar for the Scotland Yard team, and they retired there with the papers from Anderton House. Then all was quiet until the arrival of Emmy and James, in high spirits and roaring with laughter. They had, it seemed, persuaded Major Manciple and his shop-crashing wife Violet, together with the retired Bishop of Bugolaland, the Major's elder brother, to come and dine that evening. Well, three more dinners were better than nothing.

"James will be paying, bless him," Emmy said infuriatingly. "The Manciples are as poor as church mice."

With no thought of being prophetic, I swear, I told myself that there might well be a second murder at The Blue Moon.

It didn't happen that night, of course. In fact, it was one of those delightful evenings that stay in the memory long after unpleasant events have been mercifully cast out by intelligent but unconscious processes of mental selection.

Major Manciple, referred to by all as George, was a graying

man with a military manner that anybody could see was assumed, despite his bristling moustache. He was quite clearly a gentle soul, with a quiet, dry sense of humor. Emmy had described Violet to me as the nearest thing to a saint still standing on two legs, and indeed she turned out to be a still-pretty, self-effacing elderly lady whose soft voice retained delightful traces of an Irish brogue. The Character, however, was the Bishop, Edwin Manciple. Tall, commanding, and with a shock of white hair, he looked exactly like an Old Testament prophet rebuking the sins of the people in no uncertain manner. His jaw was firm, his voice stentorian, and his manner one that brooked no contradiction. Anybody foolish enough to worship a golden calf in his presence would have been given something to think about. He greeted Henry with a crossword puzzle clue that I am delighted to say I have forgotten, slapped him so hard on the back when he got the answer right that poor Tibbett nearly fell off his chair, and announced to the world in general that he intended to have a thick, underdone fillet steak.

"Violet," he bellowed, "has become very unreliable on steaks recently."

"It's because they are so expensive these days, Edwin dear," Violet ventured.

"Balderdash," she was told. "In Bugolaland, any village chief would offer you a decent steak, even if it came off his youngest wife."

Montague, who was unfortunately taking the order, appeared about to faint, so I quickly dismissed him to get Fred with the wine list and summoned Steve, who had a stronger stomach. Everyone else had Danny's special chicken, with various starters. A bottle of rather good Burgundy was ordered for the Bishop, while the rest of the party settled for two bottles of dry Graves, one to be kept cool until needed. I tried to indicate by the subtlest means at my disposal that this would probably be wasted on these people and would cost a great deal, but James was impervious to any signals. I shrugged. This was his party, after all, and it was up to him what he spent. All the same, I disliked the implication that James was acting as lifeboat for the sinking ship. We'd had a bit of bad luck, certainly, but we'd try to weather it without my second cousin spending hundreds of pounds on a dinner party that would not really make any significant contribution to the life or demise of The Blue Moon.

When the handful of other diners had been greeted, seated, and served, I felt that I could join James's table for a glass of wine—something I never did as a rule, but the circumstances were, to say the least, unusual. Naturally, it was impossible to avoid the subject of Miss Fotheringay's death.

"The Council should really take steps to eliminate those dreadful fungus things," remarked George Manciple. "Most people know where they grow. It's downright dangerous."

"But they're a rare species, George," said Violet, and I remembered Emmy mentioning that she was a keen if not fanatical gardener.

"Never liked the Fotheringay woman myself," announced the Bishop. "No woman should have that amount of money. Gives them ideas." He attacked his steak with gusto. "Besides the vicar of Much Matchingly has told me himself that she was unsound on the Virgin Birth."

"That's no reason for killing her, Edwin," Violet remonstrated gently.

"Men have been burned at the stake for less," retorted Edwin. Turning to me, he added, "Talking of steaks, Miss Gardiner, this one is quite excellent. You might give Violet some instruction in the preparation of a really fine fillet."

Before I could reply, Violet said, with a certain amount of spirit, "The first instruction, Edwin, would be to buy some very dear meat."

"Have a little more wine, Bishop," James said tactfully.

And then spoiled it by adding, to Henry, "I suppose you'll be arresting Nigel Brandon?"

"I really don't see how I can," said Henry, almost apologetically. Reynolds speared a piece of chicken ferociously.

"He needed money and his aunt refused to give it to him," James pointed out. "Now he's got it. Talk about a motive."

"I'm afraid," said Henry, smiling, "that I can't talk about a motive or anything else. All I will say is that if Brandon put the Destroying Angel into his aunt's dish, he must be a magician—as Miss Gardiner pointed out."

"He could have had help, Henry." This from Emmy. "Somebody in the kitchen—"

Henry shot her a glance that said clearly "You of all people should know better than to discuss a case in front of outsiders." Aloud, he said mildly, "There's a lot of work still to be done. It'll all come out in court, don't you worry." And to me: "Your chef is to be congratulated, Miss Gardiner. Three stars in Michelin, in my opinion. Worth the voyage."

"I'll tell Danny. He'll be thrilled. And do please call me Susan. Unless I'm a suspect, of course."

Henry raised his glass to me. "Even a suspect may be called by her first name," he said, too enigmatically for my liking. "Your health, Susan."

I left the party then to their *crème brulée*—cheese and biscuits for Edwin, of course, which I felt sure he ordered just to be different—and to coffee, thin mints, and liqueurs. As always I made my rounds of the other tables. There were just ten diners in all, and from their voices it was obvious that they were all foreigners visiting England on business or pleasure, who had not yet made the connection between The Blue Moon and murder. Local people and Londoners—our lifeblood—were staying away in droves. Suddenly I felt really grateful to James for having arranged at least one biggish party of undoubted Brits.

The Manciples left soon after dinner, the Bishop spreading himself over the passenger seat of the little car, while George drove and Violet crouched in cramped discomfort in the back.

When the other guests had left, I went over the evening's takings with Daphne. It was a depressing job, and I reckoned that we wouldn't even have as many guests as this for some time to come—unless, as James had pointed out, an arrest was made speedily and The Blue Moon shown to have had no connection with the murder. I didn't wish any particular harm to Nigel Brandon, but all the same . . .

Well, there was no speedy arrest. James drove back to London that night, and the Tibbetts and Derek Reynolds followed the next day. At The Blue Moon we did our best to get life back to normal.

The press continued to turn up in force, but, as I said, Daphne coped beautifully with them, fielding them without antagonizing them too much. Under the strict British law of *sub judice* that allows no public discussion of matters pending before a court, none of the papers actually accused Nigel Brandon of having killed his aunt, but it was all there between the lines. Long interviews with him appeared, together with pictures of Miss Fotheringay (very flattering and taken many years ago), Anderton House, and The Blue Moon. Within a week, there couldn't have been a person in the country who did not know that a diner at our restaurant had been poisoned.

And, curiously enough, after a few days James was proved perfectly right. We started to get fuller than ever. It was a different and less desirable crowd of people—sensation seekers rather than serious food lovers—but they filled the tables, and they paid.

James drove down on Sunday, kissed me lightly, said, "I told you so," and went off again. Four days later Nigel Brandon and Pierre Leblanc were arrested and charged jointly with the murder of Miss Flora Fotheringay.

I can't pretend that I felt particularly sorry for Nigel Brandon, but I was really upset about Pierre. In fact, we all were—not least Danny, who had sponsored and trained him. Of course, it was impossible to find out anything definite about the police evidence, but rumors were flying around the village that Tibbett had found some sort of incriminating evidence at Anderton House—something like a note offering Pierre a substantial sum to get hold of the fungus and put it into Miss Fotheringay's meal.

It sounded a very thin story to me. If any such note had been found, it would have been among Pierre's papers, not at Anderton House, and unless Pierre was feebleminded—which he wasn't—he would have destroyed it long before he went out and gathered the *Amanita phalloides*. Unless, of course, he had kept it in order to blackmail Brandon. Yes, that was a possibility. What was absolutely unbelievable was that a copy should have been found at Miss Fotheringay's house.

I knew from old Mrs. Birch, Pierre's landlady, that the police had searched his room only once, and that on the night of the murder. She didn't know if they had taken anything away with them, but if they had found such a note they would surely have arrested the two men at once. Besides, to anybody who knew Pierre, the whole story was utterly incredible. As so often, I decided, rumor had lost its head and was talking nonsense.

I went to see Pierre in the county jail. Naturally, the poor boy was distraught. I told him we were all convinced of his innocence, and that his job would be waiting for him as soon as the wretched business was cleared up. One good thing was that his parents had come over from France to support him, and it turned out that they were pretty well off and had already engaged excellent lawyers for their son's defense.

On a more practical note, I have to admit that the quality of our sauces deteriorated. Danny was trying to train Mike and we had taken on a boy from the village called Bert—but he was a complete novice, and we were getting more popular than ever.

As I said earlier, the new customers were less discriminating than our previous clientele, but since the arrest more and more old customers were coming back.

After all, *sub judice* or not, they all knew in their hearts that the motive had been greed for money, quite unconnected with The Blue Moon, and that the one staff member implicated was safely behind bars. Brandon and Pierre made brief appearances in court, at which the prosecution gave nothing away. A date for the trial was set for several months ahead, and things slowly returned to normal.

With the early coming of spring, the days grew longer, and already by March we were able to serve lunches and drinks in the garden, where the lawn sloped down to the slow-flowing River Dan. This was exactly what I had envisioned that previous April when James and I had seen The Blue Moon for the first time. The Golden Goose had done good business in the wintery weather, but now Mr. Pargeter was in a distinctly one-down position. He was slap in the middle of the village street and he had no garden, let alone the river. His cheerful fire and horse brasses were going to do him less and less good as the summer approached.

I had told James that I could run The Blue Moon on my head, and so it was proving. Again, I blessed my parents who had been so generous in providing me with this expertise. Apart from the pending trial, which seemed to keep on being adjourned, the murder was virtually forgotten.

I was seeing quite a lot of James. Occasionally I managed to squeeze in a day in London, and we always met for lunch. More often, however, he would come down to The Blue Moon for dinner, usually alone, but sometimes with friends. He was obviously doing well. He had exchanged the little Escort for an Alfa-Romeo, which he drove with manifest delight.

George and Violet Manciple invited me over to Cregwell Grange for dinner, but as I could never leave the restaurant in the evening, we made it lunch ("luncheon," naturally, to Edwin). The Grange was an ugly but imposing Victorian structure, and the conversation centered round clay pigeon shooting (George Manciple) and crossword puzzles (the Bishop). Since neither topic interested me in the least, our social contact did not blossom.

The Manciples never came to The Blue Moon, and remembering Emmy's remark about church mice, I was not surprised. The Grange was full of shabby antiques and could have done with a good lick of paint, although I must say that Violet produced a very well-cooked if simple meal. Of the Tibbetts and the surly Inspector Reynolds, I saw nothing at all.

It was on an evening in March, a couple of weeks before Nigel and Pierre were due to stand trial, that it happened. Well, to be frank, nothing happened. We had our usual crowded dining room to look after, and the last guests did not leave until after eleven. I was tired, and went to bed almost at once.

I was still asleep, in fact, at eight in the morning when the telephone rang.

"Miss Gardiner?"

I thought I recognized the voice. "Speaking," I said sleepily. "What is it, Inspector Darlington? Something to do with the trial?"

"I'd rather not talk over the phone. I'll be right over."

I stumbled out of bed, grumbling a little, washed my face, and just had time to pull on a pair of jeans and a sweater before the Inspector's neat black police car drew up outside the front door. I hadn't been worried until I saw his face. *Must be some*

formality to do with the evidence I would have to give at the trial,
I thought. But one look at that grim expression set my heart
pounding. I fairly rushed to open the door.

Darlington gave an imitation of a smile. "Sorry to get you up
so early, Miss Gardiner. I'm afraid this is rather serious."

"What is?"

"There's been another one," he said. "May I come in?"

"Of course. I'm sorry." I stood back to let him into the bar.
"Another what?" But of course I knew.

"A Mr. Albert Pilkington, of Pilkington, Hamble and Trotworthy. Solicitor. Lives Cregwell way."

"Is he . . . ?"

"I'm afraid so, Miss Gardiner. He and his wife dined here
last night. He was taken violently ill around three o'clock in
the morning and died in hospital an hour later. The autopsy
has shown that he ingested *Amanita phalloides* some hours
earlier."

We looked at each other in horrified despair. Darlington
went on. "I'm afraid we'll have to go through your trash cans
and swill buckets, Miss Gardiner. I presume nothing has been
removed since last night."

"No. Nothing."

"I'll get my chaps on to it, then." He stuck his head out of
the front door and spoke to two constables whom I hadn't
noticed were waiting in the car. The driver immediately set off
toward the back door.

"I'll open up the kitchen," I said. "But they'll find the bins
in the yard outside."

When I came back, Darlington had his inevitable notebook
open in his hand. Reading from it, he said, "Mrs. Pilkington
says that her husband ordered French onion soup, followed by
veal chasseur and a chocolate mousse. She also had the soup,
then roast beef and trifle. Finally they both had coffee and
mint chocolates. They drank half a bottle of your house Bur-

gundy between them." He closed his notebook with a snap. "Now, I don't say I'm any sort of a gourmet cook, but—"

"All right. No need to rub it in. Any dish described as 'chasseur' always has mushrooms in it."

"That's what I was given to understand, Miss Gardiner."

They found the traces of the Destroying Angel fungus in one of the swill buckets where uneaten remnants of meals were thrown away by the washers-up. When I say "they," I don't mean Darlington's constables, of course. I mean the forensic scientists at the laboratory to which the stuff was sent for analysis.

The pattern was sickeningly familiar. The remains of *Amanita phalloides* were so small as to make it unlikely that they came from more than one dish, and half a dozen other guests had eaten the same thing, with no ill effects. Mr. Pilkington had had the last portion of the dish.

I knew already—as did everyone who read the papers in the Fotheringay case—that the Destroying Angel was the deadliest of all poisonous fungi in Britain. That there was no antidote and that it was 97 percent fatal. Also, that it was a slow-acting poison (except in the rare case of Miss Fotheringay) so that poor Mr. Pilkington had developed the symptoms at just about the expected time after the meal.

What was worse was that Nigel Brandon and Pierre Leblanc were clearly out of it, having been in prison. Either this was a copycat murder, or there was an evil and apparently random killer, responsible for both deaths, going freely about his or her business at The Blue Moon.

CHAPTER
8

James more or less dead-heated at The Blue Moon at half-past ten with Henry Tibbett and Inspector Reynolds. (Emmy, Henry told me, was staying at Cregwell with the Manciples.) Henry had, of course, been assigned to the case as a result of his connection with the previous murder.

We went through the now-familiar routine of questions. Danny, Mike, Mike's new assistant Bert, Montague (who had had the bad luck once again to serve the fatal meal), Fred, Daphne, and Ali—lucky Steve had been off duty. The answers were precisely the same as before—indignant protests of ignorance and innocence. After a sandwich lunch, the Scotland Yard contingent went off to the Pilkington house in Upper Thorpe, just outside Cregwell, and suddenly The Blue Moon grew very quiet. Once again, of course, the kitchen and restaurant were closed for the day.

James found me in my office, and to my everlasting shame I was finally in tears. He came over at once and put his arms round me.

"Poor darling Susan," he said. His voice was a bit muffled,

because his face was buried in my hair. "Don't cry. Please don't cry. Everything is going to be all right."

"It isn't," I said, sobbing. "It can never be right now. I'm finished, and we may as well admit it."

"I'm certainly not going to admit it," James said with spirit. He had lifted his face from my hair, and now he put his hand under my chin and tilted it upward. Then he kissed me, long and hard, until I was gasping for breath. "You little idiot. You're going to forget all about The Blue Moon and murders and Destroying Angels. You're going to marry me."

I wanted to fling my arms around him and shout for joy— "Oh, *yes*! Yes, please!" But I didn't. I disengaged myself from his embrace and said shakily, "No, I'm not."

"You must have known that I fell in love with you the very first moment I saw you in Prothero's office. And I thought—I hoped—that you felt the same about me."

"I don't like charity," I said.

"What on earth do you mean, charity? I've told you, my darling—I love you."

I held out my hands to him. "James," I said, "I've got to be absolutely frank about this. I don't know whether or not I love you now." That was true: I was in love, but was it with the man or with the sense of comfort and security he brought with him? "But I think I could love you. And it was unfair to say that about charity. I apologize."

"Then what . . . ?"

"You caught me at a bad moment. We Gardiners have the most wicked sense of pride, as you must know. Look at poor old Uncle Sebastian hanging on to that monstrous house that he couldn't afford. Well, I must have inherited something from him in the way of a stubborn character, I suppose. I'm hanging on to The Blue Moon."

"All right. We'll hang on to it together, if that's the way you feel."

I shook my head. "That's not the point. I took on this place as a challenge, on my own—and I'm going to get it out of this mess on my own." I managed a smile. "When The Blue Moon is flourishing again, and the dining room is full every evening—then we can talk about . . . other things."

Before James could answer, there was a discreet knock on the door. "Come in!" I called, with some relief. I didn't feel up to going on with the conversation.

Daphne stuck her blond head round the door. "Sorry to disturb you, Susan," she said, "but Tibbett and Reynolds are back and would like to see you. They're in the snug."

"I'll be right down," I said. I didn't even look at James as I left the room.

Both men stood up as I came in, and Henry said, "I hope we didn't disturb you at a bad moment, Susan."

"Far from it," I assured him.

"Well, now, let's sit down and talk this whole thing over, Susan," said Henry.

"How do you mean?"

"We've been over at Mr. Pilkington's house."

"I know that."

"As far as I can gather," Henry said, "he seems to have been an unimpeachable character without an enemy in the world."

"Is it possible to be a lawyer and have no enemies?" My feeble attempt at a joke fell very flat indeed.

Henry, however, seemed to consider it seriously. "I know what you mean," he said, "but Pilkington was a typical, solid, worthy sort of country solicitor who was mainly concerned with wills and conveyance of property and such matters. He didn't touch criminal work at all. We went through his office, which is only a stone's throw from his house, and there's nothing useful there."

"Just a lot of papers," Reynolds put in, "that look as though

73

they've been there accumulating dust for the past forty years."

"Was he a wealthy man?" I asked.

"Comfortably off, no more. He and his wife lived quietly and were popular in the village." Henry grinned at me. "I don't mind telling you that I took a shortcut by getting Emmy to ask the Manciples about them. That's their account—and what the Manciples don't know about Cregwell and its inhabitants could be written on the back of a postage stamp." He paused and added, "In large letters too."

"Children?" I asked.

"Two daughters. Both married with kids of their own, and doing well."

"No impecunious nephews waiting to inherit?"

"Absolutely nothing like that. As far as I can see, Susan, this murder—because it was a murder, you know—was completely pointless."

It took me a moment to digest this. Then I said, "You mean, the murderer didn't care who was killed? He—or she—just wanted to kill somebody. Anybody at all. Is that right?"

"Not quite," said Henry.

I frowned. "I don't think I understand."

Henry smiled at me. "I don't want to alarm you unnecessarily, Susan, but I do think there is an intended victim. Yourself."

"Me? But who on earth . . . ? Anyway, I never eat in the dining room—"

"I didn't mean that somebody was trying to kill you, Susan. I think somebody is trying to kill The Blue Moon."

Without thinking I exclaimed, "Jack Pargeter!"

"Jack who?" It was Reynolds who spoke, clearly puzzled.

"I'm sorry," I said. "Of course, it's nonsense. He's the fellow who runs The Golden Goose in the village, and naturally he resents my success here. He'd give anything to see The

Blue Moon fail, but I don't believe he'd resort to murder. Really, I don't."

"We might have a word with him, all the same." Henry sounded amused. "Derek, would you pop down there and ask him to come here and see us. At his convenience, of course."

"Meanwhile," I said, "what can I do? In a practical way, I mean."

Henry rubbed the back of his neck with his hand—a gesture that Emmy has since told me is his way of expressing worried indecision. He said, "You could fire all your staff and start again from scratch."

Angrily I said, "You don't know what you're talking about. You've never tried to run a restaurant."

"Perfectly true," Henry admitted.

"The reputation that I've built up is based on my people. Of course, the river has always been there, so it's an attractive site, but until I inherited it, the place was an abysmal failure. And the only credit I can take for its success now is the people I've found to staff it."

"You're too modest, Susan," said Henry, a little dryly.

"Oh, no, I'm not—and in any case, I'm not being modest, because I'm proud of what I've done. I was lucky enough to have enough money to smarten the place up and reequip it, but my real contributions have been Danny, and Daphne, and Pierre, and Mike. Especially Danny, of course. Without him we'd never have got anywhere. You simply can't mean that I should get rid of Danny. It's bad enough without Pierre . . . by the way, what's going to happen to Pierre and young Brandon?"

"I don't know exactly." Henry appeared disarmingly frank. "The trial has been adjourned, but they are still being held."

"But why? They couldn't have had any possible connection with this second murder."

"The law," said Henry, "grinds as slowly as the mills of God. Just be patient."

I said, "It'll be years before that idiot Bert is any good as a *chef de partie*, let alone a sauce chef. Danny is looking for someone else in London, but he hasn't found anybody suitable yet. And the sauces are getting—well, all right, but ordinary. Pierre had—has an absolute flair for sauces. His béarnaise . . ." I stopped for a moment and looked at Henry Tibbett. "There's something funny going on here," I said.

Henry grinned. "What do you mean—something funny?"

"I've heard about you," I said. "I know you don't make mistakes. What possible evidence could you have had against Pierre and Brandon?"

Henry looked prim, but I could tell he was amused.

"You know very well that I can't discuss—"

"People are saying that you found incriminating evidence at Anderton House. I don't believe it. If you'd found any such evidence, it would have been in Pierre's lodgings, not at Anderton. And now there's been another murder. I think you've known all along that you'd got the wrong people."

"What a very presumptuous young lady you are." This time I was quite sure that Henry was laughing, and it made me cross.

"That's all very well," I said, "but what about Brandon and Pierre in prison, and poor Pierre's family—"

Suddenly Henry was not amused anymore. "I'm after a particularly nasty murderer," he said. "Just remember that, Miss Susan. The fact that another innocent person has been killed doesn't mean that our present suspects are not guilty."

"You mean, this could be what they call a copycat crime?"

Henry did not reply directly. Instead he said, "Tell me about this Mr. Jack Pargeter."

"I don't really know much about him at all," I admitted. "All I do know is that he took away all The Blue Moon's customers when he opened The Golden Goose in the High Street eight years ago. And he's been—well, I suppose I couldn't have expected him to be actually helpful, but he did all he could to make things difficult for me when I was restoring this place. And then there's the story of the haunting."

"Haunting? What haunting?"

"Oh, somebody started a silly rumor about a white lady being seen here on the lawn by the river. And then people started saying that Uncle Sebastian had murdered his wife here and thrown her body in the river. That's complete nonsense, of course."

"Did Pargeter start these rumors?"

"If he did, it was some time ago—before I inherited, I mean. He actually told James and me about them when we first came down to look at the place. But now, with *two* murders here—well, you can imagine how the story has grown. And I suspect that Jack Pargeter is doing less than nothing to discourage it."

Henry looked thoughtful. He said, "What exactly did happen to your great-aunt—Sebastian Gardiner's wife?"

"To tell you the truth, I've no idea. As far as I'm concerned, she's always been dead. I'm sure there wasn't any mystery about it. I can't even remember what her name was. I don't think I ever—" And then I stopped abruptly, because I did remember.

I can't have been more than six or seven at the time, but it came back to me as clearly as if it had been yesterday. It was breakfast time, and I was sitting at the table with my father and mother, as usual. I was eating as fast as I could, because I was afraid I'd be late for school. My mother was making out a shopping list, and my father, inevitably, was reading *The Times*.

Suddenly he said, "Good Lord, Patsy." Patsy was my mother. She looked up from her writing.

"What is it, John?"

"Margaret is dead. Uncle Sebastian's wife." I can remember wondering vaguely at the time why he didn't call her "Aunt Margaret," but "Uncle Sebastian's wife." My father held out the paper to my mother, his finger marking an announcement in the Deaths column.

She read aloud, slowly, "Gardiner, Margaret Jane. As the result of an accident, aged thirty-five—of course, she was a lot younger than he was, wasn't she?—beloved wife of Sebastian. Cremation private. No flowers or letters, please."

I hastily swallowed my last piece of toast and marmalade. I'd heard of Great-uncle Sebastian, and I believe I even saw him when I was a baby, but I had no recollection of it. As for his wife, she meant nothing to me at all.

"Got to go," I said. "I'm late already, and Miss Jenkins won't half be in a stew."

Automatically my mother said, "You mustn't say 'won't half,' Susan. It's bad English."

I was already in the kitchen cramming my lunch box into my satchel with my exercise books. Through the open door that led to the dining room, I heard my father say, "So the old bastard got away with it after all."

Again automatically, my mother said, "You mustn't say 'bastard,' John. Susan might—" But I was out of the back door by then, capering down the road toward school.

"What's the matter, Susan?" Tibbett's voice brought me back to the present. "Remembered something?"

"Oh, it's nothing, really. I mean, just a silly little incident that happened more than twenty years ago." And I told him about it. "Anyway," I ended, "her name was Margaret, and the announcement didn't say what sort of accident it was."

"So it could have been drowning—here in the Dan."

"Yes. It could have."

"And your father remarked that Sebastian had got away with it. You've no idea what he meant?"

"Absolutely none at all."

"Well," Henry said cheerfully, "there's an easy way to find out."

"You mean, there must have been an inquest—"

"Oh, I'll have Derek look up the report, but that's not what I had in mind. Violet is not a gossip," he went on, with some regret, "but the Bishop is, and so is Isobel Thompson, the Cregwell doctor's wife, who also happens to be an old school friend of Emmy's. I think that after lunch, and after I've seen Mr. Pargeter, we might all go over to the Grange for tea."

"You mean, me too?"

"Oh, yes," Henry said, "it'll make everything much easier if you come." Then, with a sudden switch of tone to the official, he said, "Well, thank you very much, Miss Gardiner. You've been most helpful."

I was sitting with my back to the door, but I realized it must have opened, and a moment later Derek Reynolds said, "Mr. Jack Pargeter, sir."

I stood up and turned round to face my least favorite man in Danford.

Pargeter was blustering. "I consider this an imposition. I don't see any reason why I should—"

"I'll see you later, Miss Gardiner," Henry said, and there was a distinct wink in his voice, if not actually in his eye. I stuck my chin in the air and marched out, ignoring Jack Pargeter completely.

Of course, I wasn't present at the interview, but Henry told me about it in great detail later on, so I may as well record it here.

It seems that Jack Pargeter started off by denying fiercely that he had any animosity toward The Blue Moon or myself.

"We're simply not in the same line of business, Chief Superintendent. I'm a simple country publican, running what I like to think is a cozy, friendly bar and serving honest, simple food. I don't go in for fancy dishes and French chefs and Lord and Lady Muck driving down from London to spend a hundred pounds on a dinner."

Henry said that the envy, spite, and anger in his voice were almost perfectly mixed.

"We do appreciate your attitude, Mr. Pargeter," Henry said, "and since, as you say, there's no competition between the two establishments, I'm sure you're as eager as we are to clear up the matter of the murders."

"It was a murder, then? The second one, I mean." Pargeter was rubbing his hands together in ill-concealed glee. "Poor Mr. Pilkington. Such a nice gentleman—very popular in these parts. I was telling him only the other day that he'd do better to stick to our good English fare instead of wasting his money on—" He seemed to realize that the remark was unfortunate, because he backpedaled at once. "Well, as I was saying, that makes two murders. Very bad for business, I fear. Poor Miss Gardiner—and after all the money she's spent on this place."

"What I really wanted to talk about, Mr. Pargeter," said Henry, "is this ghost business."

"Ghost? What ghost?" Pargeter had gone as pale as his florid complexion would allow.

"I believe," Henry said, "that the first time you met Miss Gardiner and her cousin, you told them that there were rumors that The Blue Moon was haunted and that the original owner, Mr. Sebastian Gardiner, might have murdered his wife here."

"Well, now." Pargeter was sweating. "I may have mentioned some such thing—in fun, you understand. Of course, I'd no idea then that they had any sort of personal interest in The Blue Moon."

"And I also gather," Henry went on, "that since Miss Fotheringay's death, the rumors have become even more prevalent."

"Well, it's natural, isn't it? People hear talk about a murder, and their minds are bound to go back to—well . . ."

"That," said Henry, "is exactly what I'm getting at. How did Mrs. Margaret Gardiner die?"

Pargeter looked surprised. "I thought you knew, Chief Superintendent. She drowned in the river here."

"And how and why did these stories arise that there might have been something suspicious about her death?"

"I've no idea. No idea at all."

"But living here in the village," Henry persisted, "and running, as you say, a cozy and well-patronized bar, you must have heard something—"

It was then, apparently, that Jack Pargeter withdrew from the conversation completely. All he had ever heard, he said, was fellows from the village gossiping over the bar.

Henry then moved back to Mr. Pilkington.

"You say that you knew the latest victim—the local solicitor?"

Pargeter seemed to relax. "Oh, yes. I knew him. We all knew him."

"And you advised him not to eat at The Blue Moon."

"Why, I never—"

"You just said so," Henry reminded him gently. And Reynolds, consulting his notebook, nodded.

"Well, I might have said I thought it was too expensive for these parts. As indeed it was."

"You use the past tense, Mr. Pargeter?"

"Oh, come on, Chief Superintendent. You know this is the end of The Blue Moon as a restaurant. Who wants to go out and spend a fortune on dinner and wake up dead? I ask you. Such a nice young lady too. What a pity. What a pity."

Henry then thanked Pargeter politely and terminated the interview—much, Henry thought, to Pargeter's relief.

All this time, I had been at work in my office, totting up figures, which didn't look too bad for the moment, because they included the rubbernecks who had come to gawp after the first murder and the subsequent arrests. The restaurant takings were satisfactory, and the bar had done nicely. But I decided, gloomily, that these were going to be the best figures I'd see for a very long time. Never mind. I had made a bargain with James, and I was determined to keep it.

I was interrupted by a knock on the door. It was Derek Reynolds to say that Emmy had just telephoned, and that Henry and I were expected in half an hour or so for tea at Cregwell Grange, with the Major and his wife, the Bishop, and Isobel Thompson.

CHAPTER

9

Cregwell Grange was as shabby and raffish as ever, but as the weather was still chilly, Violet had lit a log fire in the big drawing room, which made the place seem a lot more cheerful, so that it was easier to overlook the faded chintz chair covers and the torn curtain linings. I suppose if one runs any sort of establishment open to the public, one develops an oversensitivity to such things.

Henry, of course, was greeted as an old friend not only by the Manciples, but also by Isobel Thompson. She was about the same age as Emmy—I remembered that they had been at school together—but in contrast she was tall and thin, with gray eyes and beautiful bone structure that had defied time. A very lovely woman still. The Bishop was, as usual, deep in a crossword puzzle of the impossible or Sunday supplement variety.

Violet served a delicious tea in her customary, slightly flustered manner. The paper-thin cucumber sandwiches and homemade layer cake were laid out on cracked plates in a variety of colors and patterns, all of which had been parts of expensive and treasured sets in their heyday.

After a certain amount of polite but aimless chitchat, Henry began to steer the conversation toward the matter in hand.

"You've lived a long time in Cregwell, haven't you, Major Manciple?"

"All my life, except for a brief spell overseas when I was in the army. Of course, I resigned my commission and came home when the Head died."

"The Head?" I asked.

"Our father," remarked the Bishop, as if beginning a prayer. He gestured with his pen toward a large portrait of a handsome but formidable gentleman in academic robes. "Headmaster of Kingsmarsh School. It's a long story," he added enigmatically. "Tibbett can tell you. Aunt Dora's dead now, of course."

Henry saw my bewildered face and gave me the ghost of a wink. He said to George, "Then you must remember Mr. Sebastian Gardiner when he and his wife ran The Blue Moon."

"They didn't exactly run it, you know, Mr. Tibbett," Violet put in. "I mean, Mrs. Gardiner spent quite a lot of time there, but we didn't see much of Mr. Gardiner. And there was always a landlord, although he never lived in. People were easier to get in those days," she added, with simple regret.

Isobel Thompson leaned forward, stirring her tea. Her gray eyes were twinkling. "Mr. Tibbett wants to know the scandal part, doesn't he, Emmy?"

"Yes," Emmy said bluntly. She smiled at Isobel. "I knew he'd never get it from Violet. She hears, speaks, and sees no evil."

"I am not a monkey, Emmy," Violet said with dignity, "but I *do* dislike gossip, as you well know."

Quickly Henry said, "So do I, Violet. But in my job, it's sometimes necessary to know it."

Violet Manciple gave him one of her sweet smiles. "I do

realize that, Henry, and if I knew what you were talking about, I would do what I could to help."

Emmy and Isobel exchanged smiles. Emmy said, "What did I tell you? Come on, Isobel. Spill the dirt."

"Actually, there's not much to spill," Isobel said somewhat wistfully. "Margaret Gardiner was many years younger than her husband, of course, and everybody said that he had bought The Blue Moon just to amuse her, because she was so bored. They hired a landlord, of course, but at first they both spent quite a lot of time in Danford. Sebastian had a huge house somewhere in London, but they were here most weekends, and Margaret did a lot of work on The Blue Moon. She would buy up old pub fittings, like the bar and those lovely china beer handles, and she turned it into a very attractive place. As time went on, we saw less and less of Sebastian, but she spent more and more time down here."

Henry said, "Sebastian Gardiner must have been pretty well off then. When was all this?"

"Early seventies."

"So what happened, do you know?"

Isobel looked at Henry, puzzled. "How do you mean, what happened?"

"What happened to the money," Henry explained. "For years before he died, Sebastian Gardiner could hardly keep body and soul together."

"But he still lived in that big London house, didn't he?" said Violet.

I said, "In one room. On his old-age pension and the tiny rent that Mr. Tredgold paid him for The Blue Moon, which by then was only a liability."

Isobel Thompson wrinkled her beautiful nose. "Why didn't he sell the house, for heaven's sake?"

"Some people," remarked the Bishop, from behind his paper, "don't sell their family homes. Eh, George?"

The Major looked embarrassed. "It was the Head's wish that we should stay here."

Isobel persisted. "Anyhow, Sebastian Gardiner's house wasn't a family seat. It was just a house that he bought during the war."

Henry said, "Why he didn't sell the house isn't important. What I want to know is where the money went."

Isobel shrugged. "I didn't know it had gone," she said. "We all just thought that he had lost all interest in The Blue Moon. We never saw him again—after it happened."

"After what happened?"

"The accident, of course. You must have heard. Margaret drowned in the Dan."

"Silly woman fell in, trying to rescue a cat, or some such idiocy. Serve her right." This from the Bishop.

Violet was shocked. "Edwin, how can you say such a thing? I would certainly have gone in after my cat if she—"

Isobel was looking rather like a cat herself, her eyes glinting. "It happened on a Sunday night, after closing time. Nobody knows quite when, but Margaret must have gone to bed, because she was in her nightdress when they found her. She had sent the last of the staff home and was staying by herself at The Blue Moon. Or so she said."

Henry leaned forward. "Exactly what do you mean by that, Mrs. Thompson?"

"Two things." Isobel was enjoying herself. "For one, old Harry Barton—he's dead now—swore he'd seen Sebastian's car in the village that night. But Harry had had a pint or two, and was generally regarded as somewhat substandard in the cranial region, so nobody listened to him. Especially as Sebastian had a friend in London who said that he and Sebastian had dined at his flat that evening."

"Name of friend?" Henry suddenly sounded like what he was—a policeman.

Isobel shook her head. "No idea. Can't help you."

"And the second reason?"

"Well . . . there was talk."

"About Margaret Gardiner?"

"About the number of nights she spent alone at The Blue Moon."

"You mean, she might not have been alone?"

"It was only gossip," Isobel said demurely.

'Any names mentioned?"

"People talked—you know what people are, Mr. Tibbett— about a young local solicitor."

"Not by the name of Pilkington?" As Henry spoke, it seemed to me as if the whole room was holding its breath. The silence was broken by the Bishop.

"I don't know what you're all shilly-shallying about." He emerged from behind his paper like an indignant snail from its shell. "Even I know it was Peter Hamble."

Henry said, "Of Pilkington, Hamble and Trotworthy." It was a comment, not a question.

"That's right," said George Manciple. "Did some work for us at one time, didn't he, Vi?"

"Quite a long time ago, George. When he was still alive."

"Hardly likely to do it after he was dead, was he?" The Bishop, having made his little joke, retired again behind his stockade of paper.

Henry said, "Was there ever any suggestion that he might have been at The Blue Moon that night with Margaret Gardiner?"

Isobel laughed. "What a silly question, Mr. Tibbett. Of course there was. But absolutely no proof."

"So what are the actual facts?" I could see Henry opening up his mental notebook.

"The facts are that when the staff arrived in the morning, there was no sign of Margaret or her car. They didn't worry, because she was always flitting about between Danford and London. The first thing that really happened was that her car—which had been outside The Blue Moon the night before—was found abandoned and out of petrol in a lay-by on the Chelsmford road. The police put it down to joy-riders and telephoned The Blue Moon, wondering why it hadn't been reported as stolen. The staff explained that they thought Mrs. Gardiner had simply gone back to London. But shortly after that, a couple of small boys out fishing downstream from The Blue Moon found her body among the reeds. She was in her nightdress, as I told you, and she had undoubtedly drowned. Still clasped in her arms was the body of a little black cat, also drowned. And that was it. The coroner's jury brought in a verdict of accidental death. It was presumed that she had gone into the river to try to save the cat. Sebastian told the court that she couldn't swim. The stealing of the car was considered just one of those coincidences."

Without thinking, I said, "And so the old bastard got away with it after all."

Sharply Isobel Thompson said, "What do you mean by that, Miss Gardiner?"

Henry saved me from a nasty moment by saying, soothingly, "Miss Gardiner was just remembering something she once heard her father say, that's all." To Violet, he added, "I gather that Peter Hamble is also dead."

"Oh, yes. No mystery about that, Henry. He had a heart attack a few years after Mrs. Gardiner's death. Such a young man, and very brilliant too. Everybody was very upset."

"And Sebastian Gardiner lost all his money," said Henry thoughtfully.

"I'm afraid," said George Manciple, "that after what you might call the nine days' wonder of Mrs. Gardiner's death, Danford lost touch with Sebastian Gardiner altogether. I suppose he gambled on the stock market and lost. A familiar story, I fear. What about another cup of tea, Violet?"

Henry was looking thoughtful. He said, "East Anglia is becoming more and more popular with people from London, I believe."

"That's so, Tibbett." Major Manciple took a gulp of tea. "A few years back everybody knew everybody else in all the villages around here, but now the place is full of strangers—"

"Especially at weekends," Violet added.

"Rich people?" Henry's voice was guileless.

"Too rich for their own good—or ours," rumbled the Bishop. "Aha. Four down is impossible."

"Even for you, Bishop?" Emmy was surprised.

"I am the leader of leaders, I am, by the sound of it, in an armed band? That can't be so."

"Impossible!" Henry cried enthusiastically. I gave up trying to follow the conversation.

Henry, however, reverted to his previous topic. "Some local people must have done pretty well for themselves too."

The Major and his wife exchanged puzzled glances. "Local people? How do you mean, Tibbett?"

"I was thinking of the poor man who died," Henry explained. "Pilkington."

"Well." Violet was doubtful. "Of course, the law has always been a lucrative profession, but—"

George Manciple said, "Old Tredgold has done pretty well for himself."

"The ex-landlord of The Blue Moon?" I asked.

"If you can call him that. He hardly ever went near the place. Made his money in some sort of factory in the Midlands—curtain material or some such thing. Can't think why he kept on the lease."

"Oh," I said, "he told us that."

"He did, Miss Gardiner?" Isobel was interested at once. "Who's 'us'?"

"My cousin and I, the first time we came down to see the place. Apparently he was my great-uncle's batman during the war and was very devoted to him. So he rented The Blue Moon when he heard that Uncle Sebastian had fallen on hard times. I thought it was very decent of him."

"Very," Henry agreed. He turned to Isobel Thompson. "Who was managing The Blue Moon at the time of Mrs. Gardiner's death, do you know?"

"Why, Margaret herself, Mr. Tibbett. I thought I explained that."

"Yes, but you also said 'there was always a landlord.'"

"Oh, yes. Sort of. But he was more of a caretaker when the Gardiners weren't there."

"And who was it?"

Isobel Thompson opened her gray eyes wide. "I thought you'd be sure to know. It was Jack Pargeter—the chap who now runs The Golden Goose."

"Pargeter!" I couldn't believe my ears. "But he's only been in Danford eight years, and Margaret Gardiner must have died—"

"Oh, he left the district almost immediately after Margaret's death," said Isobel. "I believe Sebastian begged him to stay on, but he wouldn't. At least, that was what Pargeter said. The place was shut for a while, and the next we heard, Mr. Tredgold had taken over."

"And where did Pargeter go?"

"I've honestly no idea. He turned up again about eight years ago, bought up two cottages next door to each other on Danford High Street, knocked them together, and turned the building into The Golden Goose."

"And that was when the rumors started?" Henry asked.

"That Margaret might have been murdered? No, I don't

think that happened until much later on. Of course, Alec and I live in Cregwell, not in Danford. It takes a little while—" She stopped.

Emmy grinned. "A little while for juicy rumors to reach even you, Isobel."

Isobel grinned back. "Touché. But I really think it was later on."

It was at that point that George Manciple put down his cup with a clatter and announced that he was going down to the range for a spot of clay pigeon shooting while the light lasted. This effectively broke up the tea party.

Emmy was, of course, staying at the Grange, although she was expected back at The Blue Moon the next day. So Henry and I left together. As the car nosed its way down narrow lanes, between banks of sweet-scented Queen Anne's lace, I said, "This all seems unreal. I mean, it's not my idea of a murder investigation. Tea parties, and Emmy being here and everything. I wonder what Derek Reynolds thinks about it all?"

"How do you mean? Derek and I have worked together for years, and he and Emmy are great friends."

"Yes—but he doesn't get to bring his wife along."

"He couldn't. He hasn't got one."

"Really?" I was surprised, because the Inspector was good-looking, for all his surliness.

"Divorced, a couple of years ago," said Henry.

I nearly said "I don't blame her," but I didn't. Instead, I went over in my mind the conversations we'd been having, and at last I said, "Henry, suppose Uncle Sebastian did have something to do with killing his wife, and Pargeter knew it? Might not Pargeter have been blackmailing him all those years?"

"That had occurred to me too," said Henry, his eyes on the road.

"And when he had got all that he could out of old Sebastian, he came back and spent a lot of money creating The Golden Goose—the one that laid the golden eggs."

"Pargeter or Tredgold." Henry was thoughtful. "I wonder just how altruistic Mr. Tredgold's motives were when he took over the lease."

"You mean, there may still be something in The Blue Moon that would implicate my great-uncle in his wife's death?"

"I'm not sure what I mean," said Henry. "But it's certainly worth looking into."

I couldn't keep silent any longer. "I think that Nigel Brandon killed Miss Fotheringay for her money and that Mr. Pilkington's death was a copycat murder. He must have known something that would implicate Uncle Sebastian's blackmailer, and—"

Henry turned briefly from his contemplation of the road ahead to look at me. "What makes you so sure that your uncle was blackmailed, Susan?"

"Well . . ." I felt rather silly. "I don't know, of course—but then, nobody seems to know where his money went. Perhaps," I added, with sudden inspiration, "Horace Prothero could tell us."

"Horace Prothero?"

"My great-uncle's solicitor. He told us—James and me—that he was about the only friend Sebastian had in his later years."

"We'll ask him," Henry said decisively. "And I also intend to have a word with Mr. Tredgold and find out more about the unhelpful Mr. Pargeter."

"So you don't think I was the intended target all along, as you said earlier, Henry?"

"I didn't say that you were, personally, Susan." Henry sounded serious. "I said The Blue Moon."

CHAPTER

10

Miss Turnbull, Horace Prothero's dragoness secretary, was predictably belligerent when I telephoned her.

"Mr. Prothero is an extremely busy man, Miss Gardiner. Surely there can't be any complication about Mr. Sebastian Gardiner's will. It was probated months ago, and everything is—"

"It's nothing to do with Great-uncle Sebastian's will," I said, not quite truthfully. "The fact is that two people have been murdered at The Blue Moon."

"So I read in the papers. I'm very sorry about it, of course, but it has nothing to do with Mr. Prothero. The value of the property—"

"Miss Turnbull," I said firmly, "I'm not asking for an interview with Mr. Prothero just on my own behalf. I want to introduce him to the Scotland Yard officer who is investigating the cases."

"*Scotland Yard?*" Miss Turnbull sounded as shocked as if I had uttered some dire obscenity.

"Of course," I added sweetly, "Chief Superintendent Tibbett can always summon Mr. Prothero to the Yard for an interview and get a warrant to search his premises, but I thought he might prefer—"

"Warrant? Summons?" I had her really upset by then. "Certainly not. Let me look at his engagement book." There was a very short pause. "Yes, Mr. Prothero can just fit you in this afternoon. You and—what was the name?"

"Chief Superintendent Henry Tibbett and Inspector Derek Reynolds. What time?"

"Three o'clock."

"We'll be there," I assured her.

Horace Prothero was not exactly rattled when the three of us were ushered into his Dickensian office that afternoon, but then he was not the sort of man who rattles easily. However, he did seem relieved by Henry's quiet, almost deferential manner, and I could read his thought—*Good God, the feller's almost a gentleman.* I made the introductions and sat down on a hard chair next to Reynolds, whom Prothero totally ignored. Henry occupied a swivel seat opposite the big desk. Derek Reynolds produced his notebook, causing Prothero to avert his eyes in a marked manner.

"Well, now, sir." Henry was at his most urbane. "I'm sorry to have to disturb you like this."

"Anything I can do to help, Chief Superintendent—" Prothero spread his hands in a gesture that was meant to be conciliatory. The "sir" had gone down well.

"Miss Gardiner tells me," Henry went on, "that you were one of Mr. Sebastian Gardiner's few friends during his last years."

"Few? That's an exaggeration. I'd say I was his only friend."

"Did he ever talk to you about the past?"

"You mean his wife's death, don't you?"

"That—and other things. Does the name Pargeter mean anything to you, Mr. Prothero?"

"Not to me personally. But it did to old Sebastian." The solicitor chuckled fatly. "I don't know what sort of grudge old Gardiner had against him, but he used to potter about muttering and cussing against this fellow Pargeter. I've a feeling it had something to do with The Blue Moon, but he never told me what."

Henry said, "I think Miss Gardiner can help us there."

"Pargeter was landlord of The Blue Moon at the time of Mrs. Gardiner's death," I said. "He left Danford almost immediately afterward, despite the fact that Uncle Sebastian asked him to stay on. And about eight years ago he came back to the village and opened a rival establishment that took away all The Blue Moon's business. It's no wonder my uncle disliked him."

"And what about Tredgold?" Henry asked.

"Never met the fellow. Can't think why he kept on the lease. Can't have made a penny out of it."

"According to him," Henry said, "he had known old Mr. Gardiner in the army many years ago, and, being a rich man himself by then, wanted to do Sebastian a good turn when he fell on hard times." Henry paused. "That's another thing that interests me, Mr. Prothero. You were Mr. Gardiner's legal advisor. Have you any idea how or why he lost his money?"

Horace Prothero grunted. "Bad speculations, I presume."

"But you don't know?" Henry persisted. "He never consulted you about investments, for instance?"

"No, no. Funny about money, old Sebastian. Played it very close to his chest. Never even had a stockbroker, as far as I know. I used to twit him about it, but all he would say was 'You mind your business, Horace, and I'll mind mine.' And look where it got him."

Prothero sighed and shook his head. Henry broke the silence that followed. "Did he ever talk about his wife's death?"

"Not recently. Not for many years before he died himself. At the time, of course—"

"You knew him all those years ago?"

"Oh, yes. I was younger than he was, of course, and my father was his solicitor. But I can remember well his great . . ." Prothero paused, searching for the right word. ". . . his great distress. Funny thing," he added, and stopped.

"What was a funny thing, Mr. Prothero?"

"I hadn't thought about it for years, but your mentioning it brought it all back."

Henry leaned forward. "Brought what back?"

Prothero laughed, embarrassed. "Oh, it was nothing. Just that . . . well . . . when the news of Margaret's death was actually broken to him, it didn't seem to hit him too hard. It was later on that . . . delayed shock, I suppose the shrinks would call it."

"You were there when he heard about his wife's death?" Henry was obviously very interested.

"Well . . . no. But he called me as soon as he heard, the following morning. We had dined together the night before, you see. That is, I had invited him to my flat for supper. He told me that Margaret had stayed on by herself in Danford. He seemed . . . upset isn't the right word. No, now that I think back on it, I'd say he was more amused than anything. That's it. Amused."

Henry said, "So it was you who appeared at the inquest and squashed old Harry Barton's allegation that he had seen Sebastian's car in Danford the previous night?"

Prothero immediately became pompous. "I told the Coroner's Court the exact truth. That I had entertained Sebastian Gardiner in my flat the previous evening and driven him to his house around midnight, because, as he explained to me, his own car was out of order. That was the simple truth."

"You say around midnight. Can you be more precise?"

"Really, Chief Superintendent, it was more than twenty years ago—"

Henry did not press with any more questions. He just said, "Of course. I understand. It's only in works of fiction that people have curiously vivid memories stretching back over years." He stood up. "Thank you very much, Mr. Prothero. You've been extremely helpful. Unfortunately, though, you can't tell me the one thing I really want to know."

"And what is that?"

"Just what happened to Sebastian Gardiner's money."

"Only he knew that."

"I wonder," said Henry. "Well, we'll be off. Thank you again."

In the car driving back to Danford, I said, "It's absolutely obvious, isn't it? Uncle Sebastian lied to Prothero about his car being laid up, and he would have had plenty of time to drive back to Danford and kill his wife after Prothero dropped him home. Somebody must have had evidence against him, and blackmailed him out of a fortune. And now—"

"And now he is dead," said Henry.

"And so are Miss Fotheringay and Mr. Pilkington. And, for that matter, The Blue Moon." I couldn't keep the bitterness out of my voice. After all, I had worked very hard and put all I had into the place.

To my surprise, it was Derek Reynolds, from the backseat of the car, who said, "It's very hard on you, Miss Susan. I think we're all very sorry for you."

I half turned in my seat to look at him. "Thank you."

Beside me, Henry's voice came dryly. "The whole thing is extremely odd in many ways." Suddenly he laughed, and said, "Or else it isn't."

There seemed to be no sensible reply to such a remark, so I didn't even try one. I just looked out at the familiar Essex landscape—the tractor plows followed by attendant flocks of snowy white seagulls gleaning pickings from the chocolate brown earth—and hoped for a miracle that would enable me to stay in this place which I had grown to love and to keep The Blue Moon.

When we got home, the prospects of a miracle seemed pretty dim. Daphne reported that there would be only the Tibbetts and Reynolds for dinner. Everybody else who had booked had now canceled. She had turned down a coachload of gawpers, partly because we never took coaches, and partly because Danny was threatening hysterics at the idea.

"I hope I did right, Susan," she said anxiously. "I mean, it would have been fifty people, but they wanted a set meal at six pounds a head for three courses."

"You did absolutely right, Daphne," I assured her.

The only consolation was a note from James: *"Darling Susan—have had to go back to London, but do ring me with news. I'll be back as soon as I can. Love and kisses."*

Dispirited, I went into the bar, where Hilda was listlessly polishing already gleaming glasses. There were no customers. Henry and Reynolds, Hilda told me, had gone off to interview Mr. Tredgold at his house in Medenham. She didn't know where Emmy was—probably upstairs changing or having a bath. I asked Hilda to pour me a glass of white wine, and perched myself on a bar stool with it, feeling utterly depressed. Then the door leading toward the dining room opened, and Emmy came in.

The sight of her cheered me, as it always did. She was wearing a black skirt and a pale-pink blouse, and she looked as merry and plump and comforting as ever. She said, "Oh, hi, Susan. I was looking for Henry."

"He's gone to Medenham to talk to Mr. Tredgold. Come and have a drink."

Hilda poured another glass of wine, and Emmy came and

sat beside me at the bar. "How was your trip to London?" she asked.

"Interesting," I said. I told her what Horace Prothero had said, and she agreed that it did sound as if Uncle Sebastian had been blackmailed—whether or not he had actually killed poor Margaret, at least somebody must have had information that would have made the police suspicious if they got hold of it. Then she frowned and said, "What I don't understand at all, Susan, is why two people have been deliberately killed at The Blue Moon now—after your uncle's death. It's senseless."

"I know it is. Henry seems to think that somebody has a grudge against The Blue Moon and is trying to ruin it—with some success, I may say. My own idea is much simpler. Nigel Brandon killed his aunt and—"

Before I got any further, the outside door of the bar swung open and in came, of all people, Jack Pargeter.

"Good evening, Miss Gardiner." Of all the people in the village, he was the only one who had never called me Susan. He sat down on the stool next to me, ordered a gin and tonic from Hilda, and then said, "I'm glad I found you. I thought we might have a little talk." He completely ignored Emmy, who tactfully picked up her glass and went to sit at one of the tables, well away from the bar. As a matter of fact, I was glad that I didn't have to introduce her as Henry's wife. I was intrigued to hear what Pargeter had to say, and I doubted if he would speak freely if he knew who Emmy was.

"A little talk about what, Mr. Pargeter?"

"Not doing so well these days, are you, Miss Gardiner?"

"Business is a little slow," I admitted, "but it'll soon pick up again." I hoped I sounded convincing.

"It's the food that's done it," he said, infuriatingly smug. "If you'd only stuck to good plain pub fare—"

"That's the province of The Golden Goose," I said. "You

know very well there's not enough of that sort of custom for two—"

Pargeter sighed, with a touch of theatricality. "I'm really sorry for you, Miss Gardiner. Really sorry."

"Thank you," I said. "Everybody seems to be."

"Ah, but I'm not just saying it, Miss Gardiner. I intend to do something about it."

"What do you mean?"

He leaned toward me. "I'll tell you what I mean. I'm making you an offer."

"An offer of what?"

"Well, now, you couldn't expect to get much for this place, could you? Not after what's happened here."

"Mr. Pargeter—are you really proposing to buy The Blue Moon from me?"

"Got it in one, Miss Gardiner. Got it in one. As I said, you couldn't expect a big price—but it would be enough for you to start up some little place in another part of the country, serving your fancy food."

"And what would you do with this place?"

"A good question. A very good question. Well, I'll tell you. I plan to make it a sort of extension of The Golden Goose, aimed at the family trade. Change the name, of course. Serve teas on the lawn in the summer. Nice simple lunches and dinners. No bar as such—but I'll have a license, of course. A place to bring grandma and the kiddies. I don't see it as competing with The Golden Goose." He paused, obviously pleased with himself. "Well, Miss Gardiner, how about it?"

"No," I said.

"No?"

"I'm sorry, Mr. Pargeter, but I'm not selling."

"You're crazy." He sounded positively angry.

"Maybe I am. We'll see." I finished my drink and stood up.

"It was a kind thought, Mr. Pargeter, and I appreciate your offer. But—I'm sorry. No."

"You haven't even heard my offer yet," he objected.

"I've heard enough to know that it won't be anything like what The Blue Moon is worth."

"It's worth virtually nothing, and you know it." The veneer of jolliness dropped away like flaking paint. "I came here to do you a good turn, out of the kindness of my—"

He broke off abruptly as the bar door opened, and Henry and Reynolds came in. In an entirely different tone he said, "Well, have to be off now. Got my own bar to see to. Likely to be pretty busy, on a nice evening like this. Hail and farewell, as they say, Chief Superintendent." And he was gone.

CHAPTER

11

"What did our friend Pargeter want, Susan? I shouldn't have thought he was one of your regulars." Henry sounded amused.

"He wanted to buy this place at a knock-down price," I said.

"Did he, indeed? That's interesting." Henry sat down next to Emmy. "Hello, darling. Had a good day?"

"Not bad," said Emmy. "I went for a long walk this morning and then had tea with Isobel Thompson. I did my best to get a bit more out of her, but I think she's told us all she knows. How did you get on?"

"Susan will have told you about Prothero, I expect," Henry said. "As for Tredgold . . . well, let's have a drink first."

Soon the four of us were all sitting at the table, with a bottle of wine between us, and Henry said to Reynolds, "What did you think of Mr. Tredgold, Derek?"

"Not much at all, if I'm to be frank." Reynolds sipped his wine. "I don't believe he kept this place on just to help his old superior officer. I think he's got about as much generosity in him as an electronic calculator."

"I thought he was rather nice," I said.

"Well, forgive me for saying so, Miss Susan, but in the force we may have a bit more experience in judging people than you have."

"We get quite good at it in the hotel business too."

"I'm sorry, Miss Susan. I didn't mean to—"

"Oh, for heaven's sake, drop the 'Miss.' My name is Susan." I turned to Henry. "What did you think?"

Henry said, "I agree with Derek. I think he protested too much."

"And he must have been lying, Henry," said Emmy.

Henry grinned at her. "You spotted that, did you, darling?"

"Well, I didn't spot anything," I admitted. "And Emmy wasn't there when you interviewed him. Did Mrs. Thompson . . . ?"

"You tell her," said Henry. He sat back and took a drink of wine.

"It's very simple," said Emmy. "You told us, Susan, that Mr. Tredgold had taken on the lease of The Blue Moon when he heard that his old army friend had fallen on hard times. But in fact, he took over almost immediately after Mrs. Gardiner's death, when your uncle was still a rich man."

I wrinkled my brow, trying to remember. "Actually," I said, "I don't believe that's quite what he said. James may remember better than I do, but I *think* he said that he had kept on the lease after Uncle Sebastian lost his money, not that he had taken it on."

Henry and Emmy exchanged disappointed glances. "Ah, well," said Henry, "so much for a nice little theory. But I'd still like to know why he decided to run a pub, when his real interest was a textile factory in the Midlands."

"Oh, I remember now. Of course. He said he was semi-retired and had his house in Medenham, and he felt sorry for Uncle Sebastian, losing his wife and Pargeter walking out on him. And The Blue Moon was doing quite well then."

"I still don't think he was telling the truth," Reynolds said stubbornly.

"Perhaps not. But that doesn't make him a murderer."

"I'd better check up on a few facts, sir. Like whether Mr. Sebastian Gardiner was really a Captain in the army and Tredgold was his batman. It could be just a story."

"By all means, check with the Ministry of Defense," Henry said, "but I think you'll find those facts are true. No, I don't think Tredgold was entirely frank with us, but what possible reason could he have had for either of these murders? Tell me that, Derek."

"Search me," Reynolds said gloomily.

A heavy silence was broken by Emmy, who said, "Has Mr. Tredgold tried to get The Blue Moon back from you, Susan?"

"I should say not. He was only too glad to be rid of it as fast as possible. It was nothing but a white elephant to him. James will bear me out on that."

Henry said, "But Pargeter did try to buy it."

"You can't mean," I said, "that Pargeter would go as far as murder to ruin The Blue Moon, with the idea of getting me out and buying the place cheap? It's absurd."

Henry rubbed the back of his neck in what I had come to recognize as a characteristic gesture. "I'm not sure what I mean," he said, "but I'm sure this place has something to do with the deaths."

"If Pargeter really wanted to buy it," said Emmy, "why didn't he make an offer for it when old Mr. Gardiner was alive?"

"Perhaps he did, and Uncle Sebastian wouldn't sell. Look how he hung on to his London house. And Prothero said he hated him, anyhow."

"Or perhaps," Derek Reynolds put in, "he didn't see its

possibilities until you had put so much money into renovating it, Miss . . . er . . . Susan."

It was at this point that Fred came into the bar to announce that dinner was ready. So we all trooped off for a glum meal in the otherwise deserted dining room.

The next day Henry and Derek went off in the police car—Derek to drive to London to check up on his facts, and Henry to confer with the Chief Constable and the Chief Commissioner of the county.

Daphne was kept busy at the telephone warding off the press, whose most brash and nosy representatives had now established themselves at various hotels in the neighborhood and were writing "atmosphere" pieces about The Blue Moon and Danford. They hadn't bothered us too much at the time of Mr. Pilkington's death, because they had all the pictures of the restaurant left over from the first murder; but it soon became clear that a lot of them had been hanging around in The Golden Goose and that the locals had been only too forthcoming about the story of a possible earlier murder and the ghost of a white lady and so forth. For the time being, I had told Daphne not to accept any dinner bookings either from known journalists or from coach parties—but as I sat in my office that morning working on my accounts, I wondered how long I could keep up that policy. The economics looked bad, to say the least.

I was feeling at a low ebb when there was a knock on the door, and Emmy put her head round it.

"Sorry to disturb you, Susan. Are you very busy?"

I sat back and ran my fingers through my hair. "No. Just discouraged."

"Then why don't we go for a walk? It's a lovely day."

I hadn't noticed, but she was quite right. It was one of those bright, rinsed spring days, with a pale-blue sky and sunshine and a frivolous little breeze. I shut my ledger with a snap.

"What a good idea. I'd love to."

My little Nissan was standing in the drive, and I suggested that we might drive a little way out of Danford to some pretty bluebell woods, but Emmy shook her head and said, "Can't we walk here, along the path by the river?"

"O.K. If that's what you'd like."

As we walked along the tow path, Emmy suddenly said, "I can't stop thinking about that cat."

"Cat? What cat?"

"The one that was drowned with Margaret Gardiner."

"What about it?"

"Well . . . was it Margaret's own cat? Did it live at The Blue Moon?"

"My dear Emmy, I've no idea. It was ages ago."

"If it did," Emmy went on, pursuing her own line of thought, "it certainly wouldn't have fallen accidentally into the river. Come to that, even a nonlocal cat wouldn't have fallen in. Cats hate water, and they're not stupid. And anyway, would it have made enough noise to wake Mrs. Gardiner and get her up and out of bed in her nightdress?"

"What you're saying is that you think she *was* murdered?"

Emmy suddenly stopped and peered at the river through the trees. "Was it about here that her body was found?"

I was beginning to get a little fed up. "How should I know? I wasn't here and I was only seven at the time."

Emmy said, "We were told some boys found her when they came down to fish. This is the first spot since The Blue Moon where you can get right down to the river and sit on the bank. And the current is very sluggish. Look." She picked up a stick and threw it into the water. Sure enough, it revolved with slow dignity and began to drift at a snail's pace downstream. "She wouldn't have been carried farther than this. It must have been here."

"What of it?"

"I don't know. Just curiosity. Then there's the car."

"What car?"

"The old boy whom nobody believes said he'd seen your great-uncle driving through the village that night. What he really meant was that he'd seen your uncle's car and recognized it. But Margaret Gardiner's car was found in a lay-by some miles away, abandoned and out of petrol."

"Joy-riders," I said.

In an apparent non sequitur, Emmy said, "It's very quiet at night here. I've noticed."

"What's that got to do with it?"

"Just this. I don't believe that Margaret would have been woken by a cat mewing. But I do believe that she'd have leapt out of bed and come rushing downstairs if she'd heard her car being started up and driven away."

"Perhaps that's what happened," I said. "Perhaps she came running down to stop the joy-riders, found the car gone, and then saw the poor cat in the river. How about that for a theory?"

Emmy grinned at me. "Not bad."

"But you don't believe it."

"I never said that. Come on, let's get walking."

By lunchtime, Henry was back with great news. The police had withdrawn the case against Pierre Leblanc and he was out of prison. Nigel Brandon, however, was still being held without bail.

When I tried to question Henry about it, he simply said, "Lack of evidence in Pierre's case." And then shut up like a clam.

"Well," I said, "that's good news in more ways than one."

"What do you mean?" Emmy asked.

"I mean I can now let that hopeless Bert go. And Montague, come to that. With no customers, we don't need three waiters *and* Fred."

Henry gave me a sharpish look. "When you say 'let go' . . . ?"

"In Bert's case, I mean 'fire,' of course. But, praise be, Montague actually wants to go. He asked me yesterday."

"I'm afraid I can't allow that," said Henry, far too pompously for my liking.

"Oh, you can't, can't you?" I was cross, and in any case I had stopped thinking of Henry as a policeman. More like one of the family. "I happen to be running this so-called restaurant, and I simply can't afford three waiters. Montague is the least useful of the lot, and he's actually handed in his resignation. What do you mean, you can't allow it?"

Henry smiled, conciliatory. "I'm sorry, Susan. Of course Montague can leave your employment. But he must not leave Danford."

"Suppose he can't find another job here. Are you proposing to pay his wages?"

"I wish I could." Henry sounded amused. "But let's look on the bright side. I have a feeling that Jack Pargeter will find a place for him at The Golden Goose."

"I very much doubt," I said, "that what Montague has in mind is a move from The Blue Moon to The Golden Goose. His particular golden goose will be a rich lady of a certain age, requiring masculine company—possibly in the south of France or on a cruise."

"If that's so, I'm afraid it will have to wait," Henry said with perfect equanimity. "Don't worry, Susan. I'll have a word with him."

I can only assume that Henry did just that, because when I paid Montague off and handed him his social security card that evening, he was in a filthy temper. I couldn't help being a bit inquisitive.

"I hope you're off to a good new job, Montague," I said.

"Hope nothing." Montague's voice was showing streaks of the underlying Cockney. "Got to go serving ruddy frozen pizzas at the Gee-Gee." This was the local name for Pargeter's establishment. "Bloody Tibbett," he added, under his breath.

"Never mind," I said. "I expect she'll wait. What did you tell her?"

He shot me a furious look but couldn't resist unburdening himself. "That my dad had died," he muttered. "She's changing the reservations." Then, realizing that he had said too much, he grabbed his pay envelope and flounced out of the office.

When we gathered in the bar later, Derek Reynolds was recounting, with a touch of gloom, that Tredgold's story checked out perfectly. Sebastian Gardiner had indeed been a wartime Captain in a fairly undistinguished county regiment, and Private Ernest Tredgold had been his batman during and after the D-Day invasion. Not that Uncle Sebastian had been exactly in the thick of the fighting. Nevertheless, it represented a creditable enough wartime record, and there was nothing very remarkable in the fact that later on Tredgold had repaid his old master by standing by him when the going got rough.

"And yet you didn't altogether believe Tredgold?" There was curiosity, not censure, in Emmy's voice.

"Don't ask me why," said Henry. "My nose, I expect." He rubbed the organ in question, and laughed. It was only later that I learned that Tibbett's "nose" referred to his almost uncanny ability to sniff out the truth. According to Emmy, any reference to this flair had embarrassed Henry enormously when he was younger, but now, with retirement in sight, he merely found it amusing. In any case, he had always sworn that it was a complete illusion, and that the cases he had solved had been by logic, luck, or the intervention of his wife.

All the same, I was interested when I heard Henry instructing Derek to look a little further into the affairs of Tredgold Textiles. I had a shrewd idea of what might be at the back of his mind.

Nothing else of great import happened that evening. The absence of Montague from the dining room, if it was remarked at all, was a relief. We even had two brave couples dining alongside our "family" table—both American, and neither (I guessed) aware of the fact that they were sticking their heads into a poisoner's den. After all, we were still in the *Good Food Guide*, and had been written up in *Gourmet,* and some of the remoter American states might not have heard of The Blue Moon murders.

The other thing that happened, which was of no great consequence to anybody except me, was that James telephoned and said that he would be down the next day. He knew I had no accommodation to spare, so he had booked a room at a very expensive country house hotel near Much Matchingly.

So, what with one thing and another, I felt pretty lighthearted. True, Henry seemed no nearer to solving either the Fotheringay or the Pilkington murder, so The Blue Moon was still under a cloud; but on the credit side, Pierre would be back in the kitchen tomorrow, Montague was inflicting himself, together with frozen pizzas, on the customers at The Golden Goose, and James was coming in the morning.

It was after dinner, when I was still basking in the warm glow of James's phone call, that Henry took me aside and suggested a stroll in the garden.

"Why, Mr. Tibbett, this is so sudden!" I fluttered my eyelids in fine Victorian style, and we both laughed.

"Nothing so romantic," Henry assured me. "I just wanted a quiet word."

I saw what he meant. The two American couples, with characteristic gregariousness, had joined the rest of our party at the bar, and there was a lot of conversation and laughter.

Fortunately, I knew that neither Emmy nor Derek would be at all indiscreet about the goings-on at The Blue Moon, so I let myself be steered out onto the lawn and down toward the river with no qualms.

Henry said, "I spoke to Montague."

"I know you did. He wasn't at all pleased."

"You were quite right, Susan."

"Right? Oh, about him having latched on to some rich old woman?"

We walked for a moment in silence. Then Henry said, "She was taking him on a cruise with her."

"I thought as much. He said she was changing the tickets."

Another pause. "Do you know who it is?"

"Not the faintest. Some old biddy with more money than sense. Montague had plenty of opportunity for meeting them."

"He met this one here," said Henry. "You're sure you don't know who it is?"

"Of course I'm sure."

"Then I'll tell you, Susan. It's the widowed Mrs. Albert Pilkington."

C H A P T E R

12

James arrived the next day shortly before lunchtime. As always, he had the effect of lifting everybody's spirits just by being there. Well, to be honest, it was also heartening when he booked two tables for six people each for the evening—friends of his who were coming down from London. The news sent Danny scurrying around for extra supplies for a special—no mushrooms, of course, that was understood. It happened that the local fishmonger had a new arrival of exquisite spit-fresh salmon trout, so Danny was able to welcome Pierre back to the fold with a massive order for hollandaise, sauce verte, and other delights. Meanwhile James persuaded me—it didn't take much arm-twisting—to leave The Blue Moon to its own devices and drive with him to his stately home hotel for lunch.

As we wove our way in the Alfa between the flat fields which stretched to the horizon, I brought James up to date on the cases. Not that there was a lot to tell. He was delighted at the news of Pierre's release, remarking that we should now get some decent sauces with our dinners. He laughed heartily at the news that Montague's latest conquest was the comfortably upholstered Mrs. Pilkington.

"You don't think it might have a bearing on the murder, do you, James? I mean—"

He laughed even louder. "My dear Susan, if you think that even a halfwit like Nora Pilkington would kill her husband just to go on a cruise with a creep like Montague, with or without his toupee, you must be really round the bend."

Surprised, I said, "It sounds as if you know the lady, James."

James grinned. 'Just a passing acquaintance. Her husband did a small job for a client of mine who was selling some property here. Anyway, she couldn't possibly have doctored old Pilkington's dinner, could she?"

"I don't see how," I agreed, "but suppose she and Montague were in it together?"

But James just brushed any such notion aside, telling me to be my age, and didn't I realize that the Montagues of this world simply lay in wait for the Mrs. Pilkingtons to drop into their laps? "Remember Mrs. Wentworth Brewster?"

"I don't think I know her."

"Bless you, my adorable infant. I don't suppose you are old enough to remember Noël Coward."

"Of course I remember Noël Coward," I said, nettled. "There's no need to go on as though you were my uncle, or something."

Suddenly serious, James said, "I'm not your uncle. I hope I may be something—one day." I didn't find out until much later about Mrs. Wentworth Brewster, by which time it didn't really matter.

Funnily enough, the only item of news that seemed to intrigue James was Jack Pargeter's bid for The Blue Moon, which I mentioned more or less in passing.

"He actually made you an offer for it?" For a split second

James's eyes came off the road as he shot a sideways look at me.

"He didn't get as far as mentioning figures," I said. "I didn't let him. But there's no doubt that he wanted to get the place cheap. I can't believe that he really wants it. Perhaps what he said was true."

"What did he say?"

"Well—that he was doing me a favor, offering to take a virtually unsalable property off my hands. I soon put him right on that one."

There was a little silence and then James said, "You are really sure, are you, Susan?"

"Sure about what?"

"Look, I'm not suggesting for a moment that you should sell out to a rogue like Pargeter. But—look at it this way. The Blue Moon has given you absolutely marvelous experience as far as running a country restaurant is concerned. But it has also brought you a whole lot of trouble and heartbreak. Suppose— just suppose—that you got a really handsome offer for it? Mightn't it be a good thing to write all this off to experience and start up somewhere quite new, away from all the—"

He must have sensed that I was looking at him. I was studying that quirky, attractive profile, trying to fathom what lay behind it. I said, "You're wasting your breath, Cousin James. Only the two inevitables—death or taxes—could shift me from The Blue Moon."

At once, his face broke into that marvelous smile. "Bravo, Susan," he said. Then: "Forgive me. I had to play devil's advocate for a moment. Of course, we'll never give up The Blue Moon."

"We?"

"Oh, didn't I mention it, darling? We're getting married. Just a quiet wedding, but you're invited."

"James, I—"

"Here we are."

The car was turning into a driveway, between impressive heraldic gates. It was not, actually, a very long drive, and I doubted if the gates had originally belonged to the pretty but greatly restored Queen Anne house that now revealed itself, standing on a small rise that would undoubtedly have been called a hill in these parts.

James took his left hand off the steering wheel for long enough to give mine a quick squeeze. "You are going to marry me, you know. It's just a matter of time. Believe me." He braked the Alfa to a stop outside the front door. "Now come in and meet some of my disreputable friends."

I can't really remember much about that lunch. The hotel seemed to have been taken over by James and his eleven friends—the ones who were coming to dine at The Blue Moon, and who certainly weren't driving up from London that evening. They were all there in force, and they made me feel woefully inadequate. I mean, everybody seemed to have *done* something. Written a book or produced a film or designed sets for television or brought off some smashing merger in the City.

I never really got all their names, but there was a young man called Julian who had written a best-seller, a rehash of a real-life murder; a stocky, rather ugly redheaded girl called Amanda who designed jewelry, much of which she was wearing; an exceptionally lovely blonde called Sylvia, who looked like a fashion model but who was, surprisingly, one of the financial wizards. And so on.

I hardly saw James, who simply introduced me as "my beautiful cousin Susan" and left me to cope. It very soon became obvious that running a country restaurant didn't count as having done something. All that interested these people was pumping me for gory details about the murders.

As soon as lunch was over (I can't even remember what we ate, but it seemed to consist of minuscule portions of food arranged like a Japanese flower-piece and tasting of very little),

I got up from the table, excusing myself on the pretext of having to get back to work. I looked round for James, but he was engulfed in a circle of people who seemed to think they were at the Algonquin in the thirties. (And James had implied that I didn't know who Noël Coward was.) Furious and humiliated, I went in search of a telephone and called The Blue Moon.

Daphne answered, imperturbable as ever. "Blue Moon restaurant. Can I help you?"

"Daphne, it's me, Susan. I must have a car to pick me up right away. I'm at the . . . the . . ." I hadn't even taken in the name of the place.

"Matchingly Manor Hotel," said a voice from behind my left ear.

I swung round. "Henry! What on earth . . . ?"

"Tell Daphne that I'll drive you home and then come along quickly."

"It's all right, Daphne," I told the telephone. "Henry's here, and he'll drive me back. See you soon."

As we drove out through the wrought-iron gates, between stone pillars topped by lions holding shields, I said, "Now, for heaven's sake, Henry, what were you doing in that . . . that place?"

"I followed you, of course. You and your cousin."

"Are you crazy?"

"No. Just curious."

" 'Curious' is putting it mildly. You had no right to spy on me."

"Spy on you? My dear Susan, I just wondered where Mr. Gardiner was taking you to lunch. What did you think of it?"

I made a face. "I wouldn't serve muck like that," I said. "Thank heavens I wasn't hungry. Each course was only about two mouthfuls. And I suppose it cost James about a hundred pounds for the two of us."

"At least." Henry's voice was dry. "Don't you feel a bit guilty, running out on him like this?"

"It wasn't James," I said. "It was his friends and—and anyhow, it's none of your business."

"That's true," said Henry. "In a way."

"What's that supposed to mean?"

"The Blue Moon is my business. For the time being."

We drove on in silence for a few minutes. Then, on impulse, I said, "I'm absolutely dreading all those people coming to dinner tonight."

Henry smiled. "Don't be silly, Susan. They'll be getting their first square meal in a couple of days."

It took a moment for this to sink in. Then I said, "You mean—they've all been at Matchingly for several days?"

"They have."

"And James?"

"And James."

"Then why—" I bit my lip. It was all too easy to forget who Henry was, to confide in him. "Oh, well, it's no concern of mine."

"Of course it's not. Only—be careful, won't you, Susan?"

"Meaning?"

"Just what I say. No more."

Neither of us spoke again until we got back to The Blue Moon.

Immediately, I was drawn into business discussions. Apart from Derek and the Tibbetts, and the two parties of James's friends, there had been other bookings for the evening. No local people, I noticed, but three reservations from London. I strongly suspected at least one of them to be a group of journalists—but so long as they didn't ply their nosy trade, we had no excuse for refusing them. It was good to be back in the bustle of organization again, especially as business seemed to be picking up.

After I had settled details of flowers on the tables and seating arrangements with Daphne, I went through into the kitchen. There was a cheerful chaos about the place, almost like old times. The salmon trout had arrived and were gleaming and glittering in the refrigerator. Pierre was whistling merrily as he laid out the ingredients for his sauces. The local girls were laughing and gossiping as they peeled potatoes. Danny wasn't there—he took a much-needed break every afternoon. It seemed a very long time ago that poor Miss Fotheringay had been lying dead on this very floor, and the memory of it didn't seem to be depressing anybody. Henry, I decided, was being far too gloomy. The Blue Moon was going to be all right, and so was I.

From the kitchen, I went on down to the cellar to check out the wines. As I mentioned before, the cellar was a good one, deep and cool and roomy. In all the very extensive remodeling that I'd done to the building, it had needed the least: just some big wine racks, beer barrels to be connected to the taps upstairs in the bar, and a good sweep around the stone-flagged floor.

It was as I was walking over to pick out the white wines that I planned to chill to go with the fish that I tripped. I couldn't imagine what I could have tripped over in the middle of an empty floor—and then I saw that one of the paving stones was jutting up about half an inch above its neighbor on one side. I hadn't noticed it before because a spare barrel had been standing there. Could be a death trap for anybody carrying an armful of bottles. I climbed up the cellar stairs and went in search of the invaluable Mr. Matthews, who was mowing the lawn. I called him in and took him down to inspect the flagstone.

"Can you hammer it down?"

He squatted on his haunches, still chewing on a blade of

grass. At last he said, "Nay. 'Er'll 'ave to cum up and be relaid." Silence. "Looks like it's bin dun already."

"What do you mean?"

"Sumone's 'ad 'er up before this." He stood up. "I'll need to fetch moi tools."

"Well," I said, "do please fix it if you can. Somebody could have a nasty fall."

In a few minutes he was back with his battered black bag, and I could hear sounds of hammering from under the floor as I worked in my office. Then the noise stopped, and the next thing I knew, Mr. Matthews was at my open door, his sturdy East Anglian face showing as much surprise as it was capable of.

"Would yew moind stepping down to 'ave a look, loike, miss?"

"A look at what, Mr. Matthews?"

He didn't answer, but turned on his heel and led the way to the cellar steps. I followed.

He had prised the stone out, and it was lying on the floor beside the square depression where it had been. Silently he pointed downward.

In the center of the depression, right under the flagstone, lay a dirt-encrusted manila envelope. It had obviously been there for years. I bent down and put a hand out to pick it up, then thought better of it.

"Mr. Matthews," I said, "will you go up and find Chief Superintendent Tibbett and ask him to come down here?"

Mr. Matthews nodded and went upstairs. A minute later Henry was squatting beside me.

"Did you touch it?" he asked.

"No."

"Good girl." He smiled at me. "I think we'll get a snapshot of this before we do anything else."

Derek Reynolds soon joined us, complete with a small but efficient camera. Not until the envelope had been photographed *in situ* from several angles did Henry pull out a white handkerchief from his pocket and pick up the dusty brown oblong of thick paper. With infinite care and delicacy, he carried it upstairs and into my office, where he opened it. (It was not sealed.)

I'm not sure just what I expected it to contain, but somehow it came as no surprise when several photographs, sepia with age, fell out onto my desk.

They had been taken at night, by flash, and were harsh and inexpert; but it was possible to make out the forecourt of The Blue Moon, with the original inn sign, and two cars parked outside the door. Two more shots showed the number plates in close-up.

There were two more shots. One, taken through the open window of one of the cars, showed, lying on the backseat, a small, pathetic corpse. A little black cat. The final shot, for which flash had not been used, was eerie in the extreme. In the faint moonlight, it was just possible to make out the shadowy form of a man, carrying something white and flowing in his arms. A woman in a long white nightdress. The envelope also contained the negatives.

For a long moment Henry and I looked at each other in silence. Then I said, "Emmy was worried about the cat."

"Emmy is very perspicacious," said Henry. He put the photographs back into the envelope. "The first thing is to trace those number plates—but I don't think the answer will be any great surprise. You don't happen to know whether your great-uncle had any insurance on his wife's life?"

"No, I don't," I said. "But you can surely find that out too."

"Of course."

"He needed an accomplice, because of the second car—" I

began, then checked myself. "No, he didn't. Why didn't he just leave Margaret's car where it was, outside the pub?"

Henry thought for a moment. "Because he didn't want the body found too soon. He wanted the staff, when they arrived for work, to think that Margaret had simply driven back to London, as she sometimes did."

"Maybe. But why, Henry?"

"That," said Henry, "is another thing to find out." There was a little pause, then he said, "Derek and I will have to get back to London right away. I'll try to be back tomorrow. Meanwhile, Susan, get Matthews to put the stone back, and tell him he's not to say a word to anybody about this. And that goes for you too."

"Emmy—"

"Emmy will come back with us to London."

"Oh, my God," I said. "I'd forgotten. James and all his awful friends will be here for dinner. Surely I can tell James, Henry?"

"Susan, I said 'anybody.' "

"It's going to be ghastly," I said, "getting through this evening without you here, and James not knowing about all this—"

Briskly Henry said, "This doesn't sound like you, Ms. Susan Gardiner."

"I don't care what it sounds like. I just want to get out of this place. It gives me the creeps."

"You'd better get back down to the cellar and fetch the wine for dinner," Henry said heartlessly.

"You're a brute."

"Police brutality now, is it?"

"Don't laugh at me!"

Suddenly Henry put his arm round my shoulders. "I'm sorry, Susan. I wasn't laughing. I know it's not funny." He gave me a little squeeze, picked up the envelope, and was gone.

The evening didn't turn out to be so bad after all. James and his friends were a merry crowd, and nobody mentioned my early disappearance after lunch. Well, nobody except James, who came briefly to my office before dinner, when the others were having cocktails in the bar. He put his arm round my shoulders and said, "I'm sorry, Susan."

"About what?"

"You know very well."

"Don't give it another thought. I just had to get back here, that's all."

"I know you did. I'm still sorry."

And then he was gone, like Henry Tibbett. It occurred to me that it had been the same with both of them—to say they were sorry and then disappear. Oh, well.

The telephone rang at about nine o'clock, just as the earliest diners were leaving and the latest arriving. I took it in my office—the telephone in the hallway outside the bar was too public.

"Susan? Henry here. I thought you'd like to know that it's confirmed. The two number plates were those of Margaret and Sebastian Gardiner."

"Of course they were." I said. "The question is, who took the photographs? And who used them to blackmail my uncle out of everything he had in the world?"

"We still have to find that out." said Henry. "How is the evening going?"

"Pretty well, thanks."

"I'm glad. See you tomorrow."

CHAPTER

13

Henry and Derek came back to The Blue Moon after lunch the next day. To my disappointment, Emmy was not with them. Apparently she had decided that there was no way she could pretend a valid excuse for her presence, and in any case she had a meeting in London of some sort of child-welfare charity in which she took an active part. It was only when I saw the two men alone in the black car that I realized what a good friend she had become, and how much I would miss her.

Henry came straight into my office and sat down.

"The pieces are beginning to fall into place, Susan. And I'm afraid the jigsaw isn't making a very pretty picture."

"You saw Prothero?"

"I did." Henry laughed, shortly and without much amusement. "He reminded me of a neurotic blimp who sees somebody approaching with a hatpin."

"You think he was involved?"

"He certainly knows more about what went on twenty years ago than he'll admit. It must have been a nasty shock to him—my visit this morning, I mean. All this time, he's been leading a comfortable, prosperous, and blameless life. He'd probably forgotten all about The Blue Moon and what happened there until old Sebastian died, and he had to unearth the will. Anyhow, he doesn't deny that Sebastian Gardiner had insured his wife's life for half a million pounds—which was worth a very great deal more then than it is now. She was much younger than he was. She was almost certainly being unfaithful to him—and even if she wasn't, the whole neighborhood believed that she was, so I've no doubt her husband did too. The temptation to do away with her must have been very great."

"But not excusable."

"Of course not. It was quite cleverly thought out. Prothero was to provide the alibi—ready to swear that your great-uncle never left London. But Sebastian still needed an accomplice down here—someone to slip a drug into Margaret's food or drink and to dispose of her car. We think that was done to delay the finding of the body, so that there would be no trace of the drug left.

"There were several possibilities: Tredgold, his faithful onetime batman; or Pargeter, The Blue Moon's landlord; or maybe somebody else. The fact is that whoever it was decided not to be content with whatever Gardiner offered to pay him. He meant to do some fancy blackmailing and get the whole half million. So he brought his little camera along. He must have taken the flash shots while Sebastian was inside the building, collecting his drugged wife. Of course he couldn't use it for the last one."

I shivered. "It's horrible," I said. "I hate to think that he was my great-uncle. And I hate even more that I've inherited this place from him."

"You mustn't think like that, Susan." Henry spoke kindly, but very firmly. "Now that we've got the pictures, the thing to do is to clear up this ancient mystery and get the criminal behind bars. Then the attacks on this place will stop."

"I don't see why people should be getting killed here now, after all these years."

"Because," said Henry, "with Sebastian dead, the blackmailer was desperate to get hold of those photographs and destroy them. Which meant getting hold of The Blue Moon."

"Then," I said, "it *has* to be Pargeter. If it had been Tredgold—he was landlord here. He could have dug up the photos and burned them at any time. Isn't that so?"

Carefully Henry said, "I agree that this seems to let Tredgold out. But Pargeter, as I said, may not be the only other candidate."

"He tried to get me to sell The Blue Moon to him," I pointed out.

"Perfectly true," Henry conceded. "All the same, I think I'll do a little more ferreting around. Well, I must be off. Work to do." At the door, he paused. "You will look after yourself, won't you, Susan?"

"I don't know why you keep saying that. I'm in no danger."

"I hope you're right," said Henry.

After that, life went on pretty smoothly for a while. I didn't see anything of Henry, Derek, or Emmy. James called a few times from London, saying he was frightfully busy and couldn't get away from the office, but would come as soon as he could. The only excitement was that Nigel Brandon's case came up in court, and the prosecution offered no evidence. So of course he was set free.

My reaction to that was, first, that he was an extraordinarily lucky young man; and second, that I was not too happy to think of him being at large and probably in the vicinity—of course, he would now come into his inheritance, which included Anderton House. I suppose this was silly of me, since if he had been guilty of poisoning his aunt, he would have no reason for any further homicidal activities. He had got what he wanted. Nigel Brandon could have had nothing to do with the events of twenty years ago.

Meanwhile, business was beginning to pick up. I had always expected to do my briskest trade in the summer, and as May progressed, I suddenly had an idea.

I knew that the public has a notoriously short memory, and by June Mr. Pilkington's death would have long since ceased to be news—especially as no arrest had been made to keep the story alive. The weather was getting better and better, and I thought back to the great and relatively uncrowded days of Wimbledon, when the strawberries and cream and champagne were consumed in leisured quantities and were almost as great an attraction as the tennis. I laid my plans with an enthusiastic Danny, and then sent out invitations to the food critics of all the newspapers and magazines, announcing the opening in June of The Blue Moon's sensational summer weekend buffet lunch.

I should explain that during our first year we had concentrated on dinners, and, while lunch was available, it was a simple and restricted menu. Now I was determined to change all that, at least on Saturdays and Sundays.

Naturally, I told James about my plans. At first he seemed a little dubious. "Can you really manage it, as well as your evening trade, Susan?"

"Of course I can. And I think we'll get a good press. You must come, James. Don't say you can't—it's a Saturday, after all."

"If you're determined to go ahead—of course I'll be there. Can I bring a party?"

"The more the merrier," I assured him.

Thank goodness, the great day was as sunny and lovely as all the other days that week. Mr. Matthews and a cheery gang from the village erected a huge red-and-white striped marquee on the lawn, and by midday Danny and his staff had prepared and laid out a stunning buffet on white-clothed tables under the canvas. There were strawberries and cream, of course, but also caviar, smoked salmon, smoked eels, lobster, thin-sliced cold beef, quails in aspic, spring chicken boned and glazed with tarragon, parsleyed ham—you name it, we had it. Together with every imaginable sort of salad, artichoke bottoms, hearts of palm—the lot. There were iced soups to start with and a big dessert board to supplement the strawberries. Every couple got a half bottle of champagne to start them off.

The lawn was scattered with white-painted wrought-iron tables and chairs, and discreet tapes played Mozart, Strauss (both Johann and Richard), and Chopin in the background. The press, of course, paid nothing, but everybody else paid a great deal—not only for the excellence of the food and wine, but because I had announced that the number of lunches every weekend would be strictly limited, to avoid overcrowding.

It was a huge success, as I had felt sure it would be. There's nothing like charging the earth and limiting bookings to bring in the right sort of custom—so long as you make sure that the quality is really first rate. The journalists, quite literally, ate it up.

That first day, James showed up with a party of eight. I recognized a few faces from his previous dinner party, but there seemed to be fewer of the artistic group and more of the financial types. Including Sylvia. Of course, I was too busy to pay special attention to them, but as I passed as usual among the tables to make sure all was well, a florid-faced, opulent man at James's table was saying, in an American accent, "Such a pity. A place like this—"

I stopped. What could he mean? I took a deep breath and said, "I do hope everything is all right?"

"Miss Gardiner!" The man went even redder, and I saw James pressing his napkin to his mouth to hide his amusement. "Everything is perfect, Miss Gardiner. Just perfect."

James said, "May I introduce John H. Deitweiler the Third, Susan. From New York." He spoke as if I should have known the name. It was only later I found out that the man was one of the richest financiers in the States. James went on, with a suggestion of a twinkle in his eye, "He was just saying what a pity it was that he couldn't transport this place lock, stock, and barrel to America."

"That's right," Mr. Deitweiler said hastily.

I smiled. "Well, he can't. Sorry, Mr. Deitweiler, The Blue Moon isn't for sale—as my cousin James very well knows." I passed on to the next table.

I could sense through the back of my head that a slightly strained silence had fallen at James's table, but by the time I could turn and look again without seeming obvious, everyone was talking and laughing quite naturally. I did notice that James and Mr. Deitweiler had their heads close together and were conferring earnestly, and it flitted through my brain to wonder what the American's remark had really meant—but I was busy and soon forgot it.

When the last guests finally left the lawn, around half-past four, the staff began the clearing-up process. I say "left the lawn" advisedly, because many of them simply moved inside to the bar.

Daphne was kept busy turning down requests for dinner reservations—every table had been taken well in advance. From overheard conversations, I gathered that a number of the lunchers had booked rooms for the night at Matchingly Manor, and I was pleased to hear not a few of them grumbling that they would have to make do with a two-mouthful, work-of-art dinner. Although, goodness knows, most of them had eaten enough at lunch to keep them going for a week.

James and his party had left about half-past three, with many hand-shakings and congratulations and promises to come again and bring friends. So I was really surprised to see the Alfa outside the front door again at half-past six. I quickly left my office and hurried out to see what he wanted.

"Wanted?" James put both hands on my shoulders and kissed me lightly. "You, of course, darling Susan."

I laughed happily. "I'm glad of that," I said. "Did your friends really enjoy themselves?"

"They had the time of their lives. This is a brilliant idea of yours, Susan. I was talking to some of the press contingent, and they were all raving with enthusiasm. The Blue Moon can't look back after this."

Tired as I was, I beamed. "I don't like counting chickens, but I do believe you're right."

"Well then," said James.

"Well then, what?"

"Don't you remember what you said the first time I asked you to marry me?"

"Oh." To tell the truth, in the excitement of that day, I had forgotten.

James hadn't. He quoted " 'When The Blue Moon is flourishing again—' "

I put my arms round his neck.

"You're being a little premature. Wait for the press write-ups and the actual bookings."

"You mercenary child." He kissed me again, long and seriously.

I wriggled free. "Not out here, James."

"Then let's go to your sitting room. Can we have dinner there—just us?"

I hesitated, then said, "Yes, of course. But it'll have to be late."

"Far too late for me to drive back to London afterward."

"Oh, all right. I do have a room free."

"I sincerely hope that won't be necessary," said James.

It wasn't.

I woke next morning with a wonderful, sleepy, happy glow. It seemed so long—and indeed it was—since I had been able to stretch out a drowsy early-morning hand and find somebody there. And not just anybody, but James. How I had ever doubted that I loved him, I couldn't imagine. I looked at him as he lay, tousled and sleeping and half smiling, and I thought back on all his kindness. Coming with me to The Blue Moon for the first time. Helping me through the backbreaking business of getting the place refurbished. And then, support and comfort when the nightmare of the murders was at its worst. Dear James. I have always valued kindness above everything else in the people I love.

However, there was no time for sentimental musings. This was Sunday, the first totally public day of The Blue Moon buffet, and even though the press notices had not yet come out, word had already got around and we were fully booked. No time to lie in bed, which was James's idea when he woke up.

"After lunch, when everyone has gone . . ." I promised, as we finished breakfast. "Now, you settle yourself somewhere with the Sunday papers and let me get to work."

It was at half-past twelve, when lunch was in full swing, that James came out of the house with a distinctly fed-up expression on his face and motioned for me to go and talk to him. I disengaged myself from the couple who were enthusing about the smoked eel and went over to him.

"Darling," he said, "the most bloody thing has happened."

"Oh? What?"

"I've just had a call from London. I have to go back. Now."

"Oh, *James* . . ."

"I know, I know. I've said all that."

"But it's Sunday. It can't be anything to do with business."

He hesitated for a moment. "You remember that fellow Deitweiler who was here yesterday?"

"The American? Yes, of course."

"Well, we're in the middle of negotiating a very important deal with him, and he just called me—wants to have another talk before the official meeting tomorrow. I'm truly sorry, angel. I absolutely have to go."

"All right. It's not the end of the world." I took his arm. "I suppose you told him he could find you here."

James had the grace to look a little sheepish. "I'm afraid I did."

"Sure of yourself, weren't you, you conceited pig."

"No," James said very seriously. "I was sure of you." We looked at each other for a long moment. "Well, that's it, darling. I have to go. But I've got an idea. Deitweiler flies back to the States on Tuesday night, so everything has to be tied up by then. Why don't you come up to town on Wednesday for a couple of nights?"

"Oh, I'd love to. But I can't possibly leave—"

"Of course you can. You'll be back on Friday, ready for the weekend. You can't work *all* the time, Susan."

"I'll think about it. Off you go, then. I have to get back on duty."

I heard the Alfa starting up in the front drive and then setting off. Well, it couldn't be helped. However, it wasn't more than ten minutes later when Daphne came out to tell me I was wanted on the phone. "Sounds like James," she said.

"Susan?" James sounded worried. "I thought I'd better call you. I'm at The Golden Goose."

"The Golden . . . ? Why, for heaven's sake?"

Embarrassed, James said, "I just looked in on my way through the village to buy some cigarettes." James still smoked, although he had promised to give it up. He knew that I thoroughly disapproved, and with his usual consideration he never lit up or produced cigarettes in front of me.

"All right," I said. "I'll overlook it this once. Well?"

"Montague," said James, "has done a bunk."

"But Henry told him—"

"I know. That's why I thought I ought to let you know. Maybe you should tell Tibbett. Apparently he had a row with Pargeter last night and flounced out, saying that he was taking the night ferry from Harwich. He may be anywhere in Europe by now. Pargeter is furious. Well, there it is, darling. See you Wednesday. Bye."

CHAPTER

14

Henry had left me a Chelsea telephone number for emergencies, and I rang it right away. Emmy answered.

"Susan! How nice to hear from you. I'm told your buffet is a huge success . . . Oh, the food critic of *The Clarion* uses our local, and he was in there last night, raving about it . . . I'm so—oh, Henry. Yes, of course. I do hope there's nothing wrong."

"Not really," I said. "I'm not sure."

"Well, hold on a tick and I'll get him."

A couple of minutes later, Henry was saying "Yes, I know. I've just had Darlington on the line."

"You didn't confiscate Montague's passport?"

There was a tiny pause, then Henry said, "It hardly seemed necessary."

"But you knew he was planning to go off cruising with Mrs. Pilkington?"

"Yes, I suppose it was rather foolish of us." Henry sounded positively sheepish, and I decided not to rub it in any further, but I must say I was a bit surprised. I mean, it was so unlike the Tibbett I had come to know.

"What do you think it means, Henry? How important is it?"

"I really don't know. Not at this stage." Once again, the indecision was uncharacteristic.

"Did he take Mrs. Pilkington along?" I asked.

Henry laughed—a welcome sound. "No. No, he didn't. Darlington has checked on that. I'm inclined to think that the lady has given him up as a bad job."

"A pity, really," I said. "She might have been easier to trace. As it is, will you ever find him?"

"We'll certainly try."

"Does this mean that it was Montague who smuggled the Destroying Angel into The Blue Moon?"

"My dear Susan, it's much too early to jump to a conclusion like that. Meanwhile, just be thankful that the inquiry seems to be moving away from your restaurant, both in time and space. If I were you, I'd get on with your job and let me get on with mine."

It was not unkindly said, but it felt like a slap in the face. I had somehow slipped into the frame of mind of considering myself a part of the investigation, but clearly I was not. As a matter of fact, I had been thinking of telling Henry all about James and our plan to get married. I had even considered asking him to give me away, since I really had nobody else. As it was I just said, "Well, good luck. Keep in touch, won't you?"

"Of course."

I had another thought. "Could I have another word with Emmy?" I really did need somebody to confide in.

"Emmy? Oh, sorry, Susan, she's just this minute gone out. Some sort of meeting, I think. Can I give her a message?"

"Never mind," I said, and rang off.

As I made my way back to the buffet and my job, I had

decided on one thing for certain. I was going to London on Wednesday, come what might.

Once again we were jam-packed for dinner, and I decided to go into conference with Danny to see if he thought he could manage to provide extra food for Saturday and Sunday evenings, so that we could have extra tables set up inside the marquee—or even in the open, if the weather was fine enough. That would mean hiring an extra waiter over the weekends, and instinctively I thought, *Montague would do it. Pargeter doesn't really need him in the evening*—when I remembered. And as if on cue, who should walk into the bar but Jack Pargeter himself.

James had said that he was furious over Montague's defection, but personally I thought he looked worried to death. Not at all his usual bouncy self. I couldn't help wondering if Henry had been at him, but of course I couldn't ask.

'Good evening, Mr. Pargeter. Nice to see you." I kept my voice as light as I could—a sort of imitation barmaid. "Can I offer you a drink?"

"You certainly can, Susan." It was the first time he had ever used my Christian name. He planted his ample posterior on a bar stool with a soft thud. "A large Scotch, please, Hilda." Then, to me: "You heard about Montague?"

"Yes."

"I must say, I'd never have thought it of him. No angel, of course—but I never thought he'd go that far."

I opened my eyes in what I hoped looked like naïveté. "But what has he done that's so awful? I mean, anybody can quit a job—"

"Don't be a little fool," said Pargeter. Hilda had put his drink on the counter in front of him, and he took a greedy swig at it. "As good as an admission, isn't it?"

"Admission of what?"

"Don't pull that innocent baby face on me, Susan. You know very well that Tibbett has practically been living at The Golden Goose this past week. Montague picked those bloody toadstools and mixed them in the food, and Tibbett is right behind him. So he's done a bunk."

I didn't know what to say. Had Henry really been in Danford most of the week, without ever letting me know? And why had nobody else told me? The staff all lived in the village. I swallowed hard and said, "I'm afraid I can't discuss anything to do with the case, Mr. Pargeter."

Jack Pargeter seemed to make a big effort to relax. He said, "Sorry, Susan. Of course you can't. You obviously know a lot more than any of us—quite pally with Scotland Yard, aren't you?"

"They've been very kind and polite."

"Yes—well, that's not what I came to talk about, as a matter of fact. It's wine."

"Wine? I didn't think The Golden Goose went in for wine much."

"Well, it's true our trade is mostly in beer and spirits, but there's a growing interest in wine, even in these parts, you know. Something to do with the influence of the posh clients of The Blue Moon," he added, with more than a trace of malice.

"So you're after a cheap but drinkable wine to serve by the glass?"

Pargeter took another gulp of Scotch and attempted an avuncular smile. "Now, you know better than that, Susan. We've had your Spanish red and white by the glass for years. No, I reckon we're going to try something fancier."

"To go with the pizza?" I'm not really a very spiteful person, but I did dislike Pargeter.

However, he seemed too thick-skinned even to take offense.

He said, "Oh, I plan to go in for more upmarket food too. Very good frozen portion-controlled dishes you can get these days, you know. Chicken Kiev, garlic prawns, veal parmigiana—you'd be surprised. Only need heating up."

"I'd better look to my laurels," I said. Wasted on him, of course.

"So," he went on, "I thought you could give me a few tips on what wines to buy—you being the expert, as it were. Now, I know you're busy, especially weekends. So I thought, maybe I could just slip down to your cellar and take a few notes of what you keep—"

It was almost pathetically transparent. But of course, he didn't know that I knew what was in the cellar—or rather, what had been there. I suppose, if I hadn't, I just might have fallen for his story. Anyhow, he was deathly pale and sweating.

"What an extraordinary idea," I said. "You know nothing about wine. My stock wouldn't mean anything to you."

"What I was thinking—" He was trying hard. "What I mean—if you gave me your wine list, so as I could see the prices—"

"Then you wouldn't need to go down to the cellar, would you?"

"I'd be interested to see how much stock you keep—"

I made up my mind. I had had an idea.

"I'd like to be helpful, Mr. Pargeter," I said. "As you say, I am very busy—or will be in a few minutes. I'll tell you what I'll do. I'll bring you a wine list, and also invoices from my wine merchants, so that you can see the markup. Then you can go down and estimate the stock I keep in the various price ranges. I'm afraid I won't be able to go with you, but Daphne will show you the way and give you the key."

He looked as if he couldn't believe his ears—as well he might. "That's remarkably kind of you, Susan."

"That's O.K. We publicans must stick together, mustn't we?" I got up. "I'll go and get those invoices. You'll find a wine list on the bar."

I practically ran into the hall, where Daphne sat at her desk, taking—or, at the moment, turning down—bookings.

"Is Fred back?"

"Yes. He just came in."

"Then get him to sit in for you. I need you. Come along."

In my office, I pulled out some relevant invoices from my wine suppliers and took the cellar key out of the locked desk drawer where I always kept it. Then I opened another desk drawer and brought out my small Polaroid camera.

"D'you know how to work this, Daphne?"

Her eyes opened wide in surprise. "Of course. I've got one just like it."

"Good. Now here's what I want you to do."

I took the invoices to Pargeter in the bar and said, "I have to get back to my office now. Daphne will be along in a moment with the key."

I stayed inside my office with the door ajar, until I heard Daphne escorting Jack Pargeter down the steep steps leading to the cellar.

"Be careful not to slip, Mr. Pargeter. Hang on a moment while I put the light on."

I heard the key turning in the cellar door, the slight creak as it swung open, and the click of the light switch. After about half a minute I went to the head of the steps and called down, "Daphne!"

"Oh. Oh, yes, Miss Gardiner." Daphne sounded suitably flustered. "I'm so sorry, Mr. Pargeter. Miss Gardiner wants me. Will you be all right on your own for a bit? I'll be back as soon as I can."

I heard Pargeter grunt something, and then Daphne was running up the steps, saying "Here I am, Miss Gardiner."

I winked at her. "Can you come to the telephone, please, Daphne?"

"Of course, Miss Gardiner." She winked back, slipped off her shoes, and tiptoed down the stairs again, this time with the camera. I went back into the office.

As I had instructed her, Daphne waited five minutes before creeping silently up the steps again. I took the camera, and she put her shoes on. Then she went running noisily down, calling out "So sorry, Mr. Pargeter! Here I am. Are you getting on all right?"

It was not long afterward that I heard the two of them coming back up into the hall.

"Please thank Miss Gardiner very much for me," Pargeter was saying. He sounded far from gruntled. "Here are her invoices. Yes, I've made all the notes I need. Thanks a lot, Daphne." And he was gone.

Daphne came running into the office. "You were right, Susan. As soon as he thought I was out of the way—right in the middle of the floor, with a sort of chisel! What on earth was he doing? I got several pictures. Hope they've come out—there should have been just enough light. Let's have a look."

Breathless, I watched the picture take shape. The light was bad, of course, but it was enough to show Jack Pargeter with, as Daphne had said, a sort of chisel in his hand, working away at the flagstone that had covered the cache of incriminating photos. My guess was that he had started the job on a clandestine visit before I took over—Mr. Matthews said somebody had been working on the stone. If we hadn't replaced it solidly, those five minutes might well have been all he needed. So here was solid proof. I must get on to Henry right away. But first—

"Wonderful, Daphne," I said. "Well done."

"I don't understand—"

"Don't worry, you will. Now, tell me something. Did you know that Tibbett has been nosing around in the village most of the week?"

Daphne is the most honest, transparent person. She blushed crimson and said nothing.

"So you did. Why didn't you tell me?"

"Well . . ."

"Come on, Daph. Out with it. I suppose he asked you not to."

She nodded, still saying nothing.

"And Danny? Fred? Pierre? All of you? You all knew and were told to keep your mouths shut?"

"I'm terribly sorry, Susan." Daphne sounded near tears.

"It's not your fault, for heaven's sake," I said, "but I'm going to have something to say to Henry Tibbett about it."

However, as it happened, I had to keep my righteous indignation to myself for the time being. The Chelsea number produced only an answering machine, and I was in no mood to leave a recorded message. Scotland Yard, predictably, informed me that Chief Superintendent Tibbett was not on duty. Did I wish to leave a . . . ? No, thank you, I didn't. Then the first dinner guests began to arrive, and there was no more time for frustration or even curiosity.

The next morning I managed to get Henry in his office. I was determined to play it cool.

"Ah, good morning, Susan. How are you?"

"Pretty well, thanks." I paused. "I understand you've been around these parts quite a bit lately."

"That's right. Last week. I visited Pargeter at his pub." Henry sounded maddeningly unfazed.

"You didn't come to see me."

"Alas, I had no need to, and I was on duty. Business before pleasure."

"There was no need to instruct my staff not to tell me that you were in the village."

A little pause. "I'm sorry about that, Susan. I thought it would be better for you not to be involved."

"I am involved, whether you like it or not. I was very upset when I found out."

"Susan," said Henry, "I wouldn't upset you for the world. You've been through a horrible time, and you've been wonderful and helpful and—"

"You can cut the soft soap," I said.

"Very well, although it's true, as you know. But you have to realize, my dear, that a murder investigation isn't a game, and that we can't have members of the public—"

"Members of the public!" I was outraged.

"All right, keep your hair on." Henry sounded amused. "Let's say, then—potential witnesses."

"That's a little better."

"As I was saying, we can't have potential witnesses in on every stage of the investigation."

"I see." I tried to keep my voice icily sweet. "In that case, perhaps you're not interested in the fact that I've got positive evidence for you?"

"Evidence of what?" His voice changed to sharp interest.

"I can't tell you over the phone. Can you get down here right away?"

"Expect me before lunch," said Henry. "Any of yesterday's buffet left?"

"We'll see," I said, and rang off, well content.

Henry arrived at half-past twelve. Being Monday, there were only a handful of lunchtime guests, and I was able to offer him a drink and a very good selection of the Sunday buffet leftovers at a table on the lawn. I had the Polaroids in my handbag.

Henry took a sip of white wine and said, "So you've turned sleuth, Miss Gardiner."

"Somebody had to." I kept my voice very light, but I knew very well that the tiny barb had registered.

"Well, out with it, young lady."

I picked up my handbag from the grass, opened it, and took out the photographs. I said, "Daphne took these yesterday. Pargeter had turned up with a ridiculous excuse for wanting to go down to the cellar. I told her to leave him alone there and see what he did."

I laid the small pictures on the table. Henry looked at them, absorbed, saying nothing. Finally he spoke. "You have a witness as well as these photographs."

"Of course. Daphne."

Henry smiled broadly. "Well done, Susan. These are just what I need to complete my case."

"Glad to have been of use," I said with a slight Cockney accent, which I knew would annoy him.

He showed no annoyance, however. Still smiling, he said, "O.K., Susan. The twenty-year-old mystery seems to be solved. Pargeter abetted your great-uncle in the murder of his wife, and then proceeded to blackmail him for everything he possessed, including, of course, the life insurance on Margaret. It explains why your uncle wouldn't sell his house. Pargeter would have taken the money off him. But if the house itself had been made over to Pargeter, then all sorts of suspicions would arise. However, all that doesn't solve the recent murders."

"But—surely, Henry, this is what happened. Once Uncle Sebastian was dead, Pargeter was desperate to get hold of the photographs he had hidden in the cellar here. He was obviously in cahoots with Montague, who got the Destroying Angel fungus for him. He tried to discredit The Blue Moon and when that failed he tried to buy it from me as an act of charity. He

142

didn't care who was killed—he just wanted to ruin the reputation of the restaurant to get me out. Isn't that so?"

Henry said, "Sort of."

"What do you mean?"

"What I said. Sort of."

And that was all I could get out of him. But the next day, the whole village was humming with the news that Jack Pargeter had been arrested. The charge was conspiracy to commit the murder of Mrs. Margaret Gardiner and the subsequent blackmail of Mr. Sebastian Gardiner. Twenty years ago.

CHAPTER

15

On Wednesday morning I drove to London in my little Nissan. James had telephoned the evening before to confirm our date, and I had been able to tell him about Pargeter's arrest, which didn't seem to surprise him. I don't think the arrest surprised anybody in Danford very much. What was unexpected was that it was in connection with a twenty-year-old crime, with no mention, as yet, of the recent deaths at The Blue Moon. However, I didn't go into details over the phone. Time enough for that when we met.

Meanwhile, I realized with a little jolt of astonishment that I didn't know where James lived. I had his telephone numbers, of course, both at work and at home—but we had always met in London at a restaurant for lunch. I felt a bit silly having to ask him for his address.

It turned out to be a duplex apartment in a Victorian house in Kensington—high ceilings, large rooms, and a feeling of spaciousness that I loved. It was furnished expensively, but—I suspected—reflecting the taste of a fashionable decorator rather than James's own. Well, that was really inevitable. He was a man on his own, very busy and certainly rich.

He greeted me with a big hug, a kiss, and a glass of cold champagne. I duly admired the apartment, flopped into a big, comfortable armchair, and said, "You can't imagine what a treat this is for me."

"You've been working too hard, darling," he said. "Not to mention all the worry. Well, thank God, that's over now. You can relax."

I grinned. "Until Friday."

"Do you really have to go back so soon?"

"You know I do. Later on I may be able to leave the weekend buffet to look after itself, but these first few weeks—"

James came over and placed a gentle finger on my lips. "Enough of that," he said. "No shop."

"Very well, no shop. So—what are we going to do to celebrate my holiday?"

James gave me a crooked smile. He looked almost embarrassed, turning his champagne glass in his hand. He said, "First of all, I thought we'd get married."

I sat up with such a jerk that I spilled my drink. "*Married? Are you crazy?*"

"I don't think so." He pulled a piece of paper out of his breast pocket. "Special license. I applied for it as soon as I got back. It arrived this morning. I've made a date at Chelsea Registry Office for this afternoon."

"I . . . I don't know what to say."

"You haven't changed your mind, have you?"

He sounded so woebegone that I couldn't resist jumping up and kissing him. "Of course I haven't. It's just . . . well, it's so unexpected and I've nothing to wear and—"

"Oh, Lord. You don't want a slap-up affair with bridesmaids and bishops and things, do you? Of course, if you do—"

"Don't be silly, James. Of course I don't."

"If you want to invite some friends—"

"No. I like it much better like this." I suddenly realized that I did too. "After my illness, and breaking up with Paul, and then The Blue Moon—well, I don't really have any close friends, except Caroline, and she's in Barbados. There are just the people at the hotel, and we can have a slap-up wedding party there over the weekend." I was really enthusiastic by then. "Oh, James, it's a lovely idea."

He kissed me again. "God, I'm relieved. I don't know what I'd have done if you'd said no. I need to be with you, Susan. Always. We should have done this ages ago. You realize that, don't you?"

"You know why I—"

"Yes, of course I do. Well, that's all over. Now, we've got just enough time to go and buy that new dress before lunch. Let's go."

It was like a whirlwind. First stop, Harrods. A heavenly suit of creamy slubbed silk, ten times as expensive as anything I'd ever owned. "Just charge it, and wrap up her old dress, will you?" New shoes and a handbag. Then off to a fabulous lunch. More champagne.

"Oh, before you order—" James lowered the enormous menu and put his hand in his pocket. "We mustn't forget this."

It was the biggest diamond ring I'd ever seen. He slipped it onto my finger and said, "And I haven't forgotten the wedding ring either. Plain gold. I didn't think you'd want any of those fancy platinum things. Am I right?"

"You're always right, James."

The wedding was hardly an elaborate affair. The Registrar was a charming, middle-age man with just the right sort of paternal air, and two young clerks acted as witnesses. James had thought of everything, including producing birth certificates for us both, to keep everything legal and correct. Personally, I found the ceremony every bit as moving as the grandest church wedding could ever be. When it was all over, the Registrar dropped his formal air and came out from behind his table to shake our hands and wish us good luck.

"One of the rather rare occasions on which the bride doesn't change her name," he remarked, beaming.

James explained that we were distant cousins.

"Keeping it in the family, eh? Well, the best of everything to you both."

We thanked him and walked out into the crisp sunshine of the King's Road.

James squeezed my arm. Inevitably he said, "Well, how does it feel to be Mrs. Gardiner instead of Miss Gardiner? I wonder if there's ever been a bridegroom who hasn't said that—although, of course, in most cases the name is different."

"It feels marvelous," I assured him. And so it did. But at the same time, in the cool light of the afternoon and away from the champagne and the swirl of luxury, I realized that we hadn't really discussed anything at all. Where we were going to live, for instance. What the pattern of our lives was going to be. What about money? I knew—or had gathered—that James had plenty; but I knew nothing, really, about his work or his business life.

"You're very silent, darling. Not having any second thoughts, are you?"

"Of course not. But we have to talk, James."

"We'll talk about anything you like. But surely not right now."

I stood on tiptoe to kiss his cheek. "I'm sorry, darling. Old practical Susan rising to the surface, I'm afraid. Let's go back to your apartment."

James hailed a cab, and soon we were back in Kensington.

He went straight to the refrigerator. "More champagne? Or something stronger?"

"What I'd really like is a cup of tea."

He threw back his head and roared with laughter. "I love you, I love you, I love you, my angelic Susan! Who else in the world would start her honeymoon by asking for a cup of tea?"

I felt myself blushing. "I'm sorry." I always seemed to be apologizing. "I must seem awfully dull, compared to your other friends." I thought of all the people I had met with James—the authors, the actresses, the financiers, the brilliant young crowd. He hadn't asked even one of them to our wedding. *Oh, my God,* I thought. *He's ashamed of me.*

"That boring lot? Don't be idiotic, my darling. You're worth all of them put together—and then some."

He came and sat beside me on the sofa, and put his arm round me. I leaned back with my head on his shoulder and felt a sudden rush of happiness. And I realized, in a moment of intuition, just why. It wasn't simply that I was in love with James—although of course I was, desperately. Especially after that magical night at The Blue Moon. No, it was something even more important. He made me feel self-confident. He made me feel safe.

He said, "You've gone silent again, Susan. What is it?"

"Nothing. Just being happy."

"Then that's all right. But I thought you wanted to talk."

I gave myself a little shake and sat up. "Yes, James, I do. I mean, we must."

"What about?"

"Oh—everything. The Blue Moon. Where we're going to live. What's going to happen?"

James looked suddenly serious. "Yes, we have to talk about those things. But not now."

"Now," I said.

He gave me a strange, sideways look and then said, "You are a funny child."

"I'm not a child. I have a job—a career. The Blue Moon."

There was a little silence. Then James said, "I somehow took it for granted that you'd give that up, now that we're married."

"Give it up? You must be crazy. After all my work—"

"Oh, darling, I know you've worked tremendously hard and done wonders—but the place is on its feet now. The murders have been solved, the—"

"Not really," I interrupted. "Henry Tibbett—"

"Let Henry Tibbett get on with it. He doesn't need you. The weekend buffets are obviously a huge success. Leave it alone, darling Susan, and start living your own life—and enjoying it."

"You make me sound like Marie Antoinette playing milkmaids at Le Petit Trianon!"

"I'm sorry, truly. I didn't mean it like that. But—well, I've got my work here in London. I have to be here. And I was hoping that you'd want to be with me."

I felt a great surge of remorse. "Of course I do, darling James." We hadn't been married more than an hour, and already we were on the brink of fighting. "It's just . . . well, I have to think about it. Meanwhile, we've got until Friday . . ."

And until Friday, we didn't think about anything except ourselves.

It was the loveliest sort of honeymoon. Short, utterly relaxed, at home rather than in some impersonal hotel. There'd be plenty of time later, James said, to have a long holiday abroad. I had it on the tip of my tongue to say that I couldn't possibly spare the time for a long holiday, but I bit it back. So we concentrated on being happy, and on being alone. James even disconnected the telephone. Until Friday, the world outside didn't exist.

But Friday came, as it had to. I was terrified that James would start making objections, saying that he couldn't leave London for Essex, or something. I needn't have worried. By Friday afternoon, we were packed and ready to leave.

"By the way," James said, "I've arranged for your car to be garaged by my people until you need it."

"But I need it now!"

"What? Isn't the Alfa good enough for Mrs. James Gardiner?"

"Don't be silly. I mean, I need my car in Danford. Oh, James—it means we'll have to drive down separately!"

"Well, don't look so tragic!" He kissed me, and I clung to him. "It's not the end of the world."

"I'm sorry." There I went again. "I know I'm being silly. It's just the thought of being away from you, even for an hour or so—"

"That is not at all silly," he said, almost severely. "That is exactly what a new husband likes to hear. However, if you really must take your car back to Danford, you shall. I'll drive you to the garage, and then I'll meet you at The Blue Moon. I have a feeling I'll make better time than you will." He grinned.

"You'll take care, won't you?"

"And you, idiot girl. By the way, you'd better fill up with petrol on the M25. She's a bit low."

I left the parking garage first and had some good luck with traffic lights, but of course the Alfa passed me easily on the M25. James, driving with blithe disregard for the speed limit, gave me a cheery wave and blew me a kiss. With some relief, I slowed down. Up to then, there had been an element of competition about the whole thing.

There was a service area coming up on my left—the last one

for many miles, as the notice warned. I remembered what James had said and glanced at my fuel indicator. He was right. It would be prudent to fill up while I had the chance.

Near the petrol pumps there was a row of telephone booths, and I suddenly had a wild urge to confide in somebody, to pour out my happiness into a sympathetic ear. On the spur of the moment, I parked my car and used my phone card to dial Emmy Tibbett's number. Four rings, and then that infuriating answering machine. "I'm afraid neither Henry nor I can come to the phone at the moment . . . if you would like to leave a message . . ."

Well, it was annoying, but nothing could damp my spirits. "Hi, Emmy," I said, after the bleep. "This is Susan Gardiner. I'm on my way back to Danford, and I've got great news— you'll never believe it. I'm married! And the funny thing is, I haven't changed my name! Work that one out."

We had already decided not to tell anybody at The Blue Moon our momentous news until we actually got there; but I still had this longing—necessity, almost—to tell somebody, and I rang a few more acquaintances on the off chance. No luck. Two no replies and another answering machine. I didn't bother to record a message, but came out of the booth feeling rather deflated.

I started to walk to my car—and stopped dead in surprise. I had parked well away from the lorries and private cars whose drivers were patronizing the restaurant, but the little Nissan was no longer alone. A BMW was parked alongside her, and a man was standing there with his hand on her bonnet, almost as if he had had it open and had just slammed it shut. He straightened up, and I saw that it was Mr. Tredgold, the onetime licensee of The Blue Moon.

He waved to me. "Hello, Miss Gardiner! Thought I recognized your car. On your way back to Danford, are you?"

"How nice to see you, Mr. Tredgold," I said icily. What

was he doing, messing about with my car? Guiltily I realized that I hadn't bothered to lock it.

"I hear great things about The Blue Moon," he went on. "Been meaning to drive over and congratulate you."

"On having two guests murdered?"

He smiled unconvincingly. "Of course, I didn't mean that, Miss Gardiner. Anyhow, that's all cleared up now, isn't it? Nasty bit of work, Jack Pargeter. Never could abide him. No, I meant your great success—your magnificent food—"

"Thank you, Mr. Tredgold. Why don't you come over for a meal sometime and try it for yourself?" He had not been near The Blue Moon since I took over.

He smiled sheepishly. "Touché, Miss G. I've been meaning to, but I've been kept very busy. Factories don't run themselves, you know."

He looked timid and apologetic, standing there in the sunshine, with his wispy gray hair ruffled by the wind. I remembered that, whatever I might feel about Great-uncle Sebastian, this little man had stood by him in the darkest days for old times' sake. I smiled at him.

"Why not come to our buffet lunch tomorrow?"

"I wish I could, Miss G., but I'm on my way to London, I fear. Board meeting at our West End office."

"Well, try to make it sometime soon. I must be on my way." I got into the car, started her up, and pulled over to the petrol pumps. It was only when I was on the road again that I put my finger on the nagging inconsistency. If he was going to the West End of London, what was he doing in that service station, on the wrong side of the motorway? Certainly, the M25 is a ring road that circles the capital, but surely he wasn't proposing to drive round two-thirds of the perimeter to get where he was going?

Mentally I shrugged my shoulders. So he had told me a senseless fib—what did it matter? And then another thought struck me. He had talked about recognizing my car. But the only time I had set eyes on him was that first day in Danford, when I was with James in the white Escort. Mr. Tredgold had never seen my car.

It was then that I became suddenly and sickeningly aware that there was something wrong with my steering.

CHAPTER

16

It happened quite suddenly, as if something had just given way. I was starting to pull to the right to overtake a lorry when I realized that the car wasn't responding to the steering wheel. I don't think I have ever been so scared. The M25 on a Friday afternoon is not the place to lose control of one's car, especially going at the top speed allowed—seventy miles an hour. I made frantic hand signals to show I was slowing down and jabbed at my brakes. And nothing happened.

This was the ultimate nightmare. The steering might have gone on its own, but the brakes as well—that couldn't be an accident. I did the only thing I could think of—I leaned hard on the horn. Thank God, that was working. But there was a petrol truck ahead of me going at no more than fifty miles an hour in the slow lane, and I didn't see how I could miss it. It loomed larger and larger, closer and closer.

Other drivers, however, were beginning to respond to my blaring horn, and in the nick of time the truck veered off onto the soft verge as I careered past him. There was a clash of metal as I struck him a glancing blow, which had the merciful effect of slowing my speed a little, but not nearly enough.

Desperately I tried to remember the geography of this part of the motorway. When would there be a hill? The rest of the traffic was keeping out of my way now, and I could hear the scream of a police siren somewhere behind me. I took little comfort from that. What could they do, except put up a barrier to stop me? That would remove my lethal presence from the road, but probably from the land of the living too.

After what seemed a lifetime, but was actually only about a minute, I saw a blessed sight ahead. A slight rise—not a real hill, but surely enough to slow down my headlong hurtle toward disaster. It did, but not much; and over the brow, the road bent downhill again, restoring any momentum I might have lost. Gathering what wits I had left, I decided to try to get the car into low gear, and then into reverse, like an aircraft landing. There was a frightful screeching from the gearbox, but somehow I managed to crash down into first, and a miraculous slowing down of speed. Of course, that's what I should have done in the first place. Now, could I get her into reverse?

A split second's reflection told me not even to try. Suppose I succeeded, heaven knew if I could get her out again, and going backward on a crowded motorway with no steerage or brakes simply didn't bear thinking about. As it was, first gear had slowed me down to a reasonable speed, although I was still partway into the fast lane and causing mayhem among the traffic.

What saved me was a bend in the road. The motorway veered round to the right, but straight ahead was an exit ramp. Naturally the car went straight onto the ramp, which bent downhill for a few yards before rising sharply to connect with the bridge over the motorway. As soon as the rise started, I slammed into neutral. The car juddered, slowed, stopped, and rolled backward into the hollow. And stopped for good. I am ashamed to say that I put my head on the steering wheel and burst into tears.

That was how the police patrol found me when they came screaming up a couple of minutes later.

Then, of course, came endless formalities. The police could not have been nicer, but naturally they had to do everything according to the book. My car was towed away for inspection, and I was driven to the nearest station, given the inevitable cup of tea, and asked what had happened.

The first thing I begged to be allowed to do was to telephone The Blue Moon, which I was allowed to do from a public telephone. Daphne answered in her usual brisk, comforting way and told me that James had not yet arrived. I blurted out that we were married—not at all the happy-surprise breaking of the news that I'd envisioned—and cut short her congratulations with the information that I had very nearly been killed when my car went out of control, that I was in a police station (I gave her its telephone number), and that I had no idea when I would get home. Then I went back into the office and began to cry again.

A kind policewoman brought another cup of tea and told me that I was suffering from understandable shock. A Sergeant asked me again what had happened. I told him that, for no apparent reason, both the steering and the brakes had failed. The car had been running perfectly well up to that moment. Had I any idea what could have caused the trouble? No, I hadn't. But I kept thinking of Mr. Tredgold standing by the car in the service station, with his hand on the bonnet. I had been in the phone booth for about a quarter of an hour. What was he doing there? How did he know it was my car? Well, I decided I wouldn't say anything about him until the engineer's report came in. It just might have been an unlucky accident.

It wasn't, of course. It took the police engineer only minutes to make sure that the car had been tampered with—cables cut halfway through so that they wouldn't give way until I was in the thick of the traffic.

"You're a very lucky young lady, Miss—er—" The Police Sergeant had caught sight of the huge diamond and the wedding ring.

"I'm Mrs. Gardiner," I said. I explained how James and I had been driving separately to Danford. "We've only been married two days," I added, trying not to burst into tears again.

"Well, now," the Sergeant said comfortingly, "all's well that ends well, isn't it? I expect we'll get a call from Mr. Gardiner as soon as he arrives in Danford."

I just nodded.

"Meanwhile," the Sergeant went on, "have you any idea who could have played this cruel trick on you? It couldn't have been a sort of newlywed caper, could it?"

I shook my head. "Nobody knew we were married. We didn't have a reception or any friends or . . . anything." I had decided to wait until I could talk to James before I said anything about Mr. Tredgold.

The Sergeant was filling in forms. "Now, Mrs. Gardiner, a few details, just for the record. Your permanent address?"

"The Blue Moon, Danford."

I could sense the Sergeant and the WPC exchanging glances over my head. Slowly the Sergeant said, "The Blue Moon? That's where a couple of guests were murdered, if I remember rightly."

"That has nothing to do with it—anyhow it's all cleared up. Scotland Yard has a man under arrest."

"Then that's all right, isn't it?" The Sergeant smiled.

"I have an address in London too." I had forgotten that James's apartment was now also mine. I gave the Sergeant that address too.

When it was all done, and I had signed my statement about what happened, the Sergeant put through a call to the police garage. "I see. Very good. Yes, I'll tell her." He turned to me. "If you can wait here with us for an hour or so, Mrs. Gardiner, we'll have your car fixed up and you can drive home. Meanwhile, there's no need for you to—"

It was at that moment that a young WPC put her head round the door and said, "A call for Mrs. Gardiner."

"Susan, darling! What happened? Are you all right? I just got here, and Daphne says—"

"Oh, James! Yes, I'm fine. The car will be fixed in about an hour, and I'll drive—"

"You're driving nowhere, you precious imbecile. I'm coming to get you. Leaving in five minutes. The police can look after your car until we come to pick it up. And, Susan—"

"Yes, James?"

"Don't ever do anything like this to me again. You're my wife and I love you—remember?"

"I hadn't forgotten, darling."

I walked back into the office about a foot off the ground. "My husband is coming to fetch me."

"Call him back and tell him not to bother," said a familiar voice. I hadn't even noticed that there was anybody else in the room, but there he was. Henry Tibbett.

"Henry! What on earth?"

"Go and ring James at once, before he starts. It'll take him a good hour to get here, and I can run you home, starting now. Go on, Susan. Don't be silly."

James sounded far from pleased. "What on earth is Tibbett doing there?" he demanded.

"I've no idea, darling, but he's on his way to Danford, so the most sensible thing is for him to drive me."

"Oh, very well. But tell him to hurry."

Henry was driving himself in the black police car, and I

climbed into the front seat beside him. As he started the engine, he looked sideways at me and said grimly, "Do you realize just how lucky you are, Susan?"

"Yes," I said. "I do."

"The odds on you being killed were formidable."

"Henry—how did you know about it? How did you know where I was?"

"I had already started for Danford when the news came over the police radio. They didn't give your name, of course—they didn't know it at that stage—but they described the car and driver, and I felt absolutely sure it was you."

"You knew my car would be tampered with?"

"No. But I guessed you might come to some harm."

"Whyever should I?"

"I'll explain that later. Perhaps. Meanwhile, I gather congratulations are in order. Emmy tells me you're married."

"Oh, so she got my message?"

"Yes. She had only gone out shopping for a few minutes. She rang me at the Yard to tell me."

"She did? Why?"

"I suppose," said Henry, "that she thought I'd be interested. I hope you'll be very happy, Susan."

"I'm very happy already."

We drove in silence for a few minutes, then I said, "Henry, there's something I didn't tell the police back there, but I'm going to tell you." And I recounted the strange episode of Mr. Tredgold at the service station, and how easily he could have sabotaged my car. "He couldn't have recognized me in the phone booth," I explained, "and he'd never seen my car before. How on earth did he . . . ?"

"That's very interesting, Susan." Henry's eyes were firmly on the road ahead. "I wondered how it was done."

"Oh, you are infuriating. Do explain. After all, surely I'm entitled to know—"

"All in good time," said Henry, with a maddening smile. "Well, so you're enjoying married life?"

"I've only had two days of it, but so far it's like the Garden of Eden."

"After the Fall, I trust," said Henry, deadpan.

I laughed. "Naturally."

"So this rather changes things for you, doesn't it? Will you sell The Blue Moon and go and live in London with James?"

I hesitated. "We haven't really decided that yet. James would like me to, but I love my work and we're really becoming successful now. I might put in a manager so that I could be away more. I hate the thought of selling."

"I'm sure you do. Well, I'm sure you'll work something out between you."

Changing the subject, I said, "How's the case against Pargeter coming along?"

Henry was noncommittal. "Slowly, like all these things."

"Well, it's a relief to know that he's behind bars."

"Yes," Henry said shortly.

"No sign of Montague?"

"Interpol are on the lookout for him. We'll get him sooner or later."

"What can you charge him with, when you do?"

Henry looked surprised. "Accessory before the fact," he said. "It's clear now that it was he who picked the Destroying Angel toadstools and slipped them into the food."

"No wonder he was thick with Pargeter, even though he pretended not to be."

"Yes," Henry said again.

The A12 highway was now unfolding ahead of us, running through the familiar countryside of flat fields where the new grain was sprouting. Before long, we came to the Danford turnoff.

Henry had scarcely come to a stop outside The Blue Moon before I was out of the car and racing for the door. It opened before I reached it, and then James and I were clinging to each other like ecstatic children.

Henry's voice behind me said, "I hate to interrupt, but do you think I could come in?"

We sprang apart, and James said, "I'm terribly sorry, but the relief—"

"Of course," said Henry.

"I must thank you, Tibbett, for driving Susan home. What a piece of luck that you happened to turn up."

Henry smiled. "Sometimes one can give one's luck a small shove in the right direction," he said. And he walked past us into the inn.

When James and I had recovered our composure enough to follow Henry in, we found him at the desk in close consultation with Daphne.

"Yes, of course, Henry," she was saying. "Dinner for three tonight and the buffet tomorrow and Sunday. You'll have to ask Susan about—" She looked up and saw me. "Oh, here she is now!"

She came running out from behind the reception desk and flung her arms round my neck. "Oh, Susan! Congratulations! I'm so happy for you both! You too, James!"

Suddenly it seemed as if the whole staff was there, and that everybody was hugging and kissing one another, and that everybody was saying they had seen it coming a mile off, and wasn't it wonderful, and the whole miserable adventure with the car just faded into nothingness as James and I laughed and shook hands and embraced and slapped backs. It was exactly the homecoming I had imagined.

But that sort of thing can't go on forever, and eventually everyone went off back to work, and Daphne was answering the phone again and accepting orders for the buffet. Henry, who had been standing quietly in the background while all the brouhaha went on, now stepped forward.

"I must add my congratulations to the rest," he said, shaking James by the hand. Then he put his arm round my shoulders and said, "And I have a big favor to ask of your wife, Mr. Gardiner."

"Anything," I said.

"Well," said Henry, "believe it or not, I'm on leave. Emmy is driving up this evening in our own car, and we'd dearly love to spend the weekend here. I've already booked our meals with Daphne, but the real point is—can you be angelic and put us up? I know you don't let rooms, but I hate the idea of that grim mock-manor house—"

"Henry," I said, "you know you didn't even have to ask. Your old room is yours. Anytime, for as long as you like."

James said, "Susan, are you sure?" And then shut up.

Daphne said, "I'll make sure the room is ready, Henry."

Henry beamed and said, "You are angels, all of you. Oh, by the way, Derek will drive up with Emmy and take the police car back to London after dinner."

It did occur to me to wonder what on earth Henry was doing with the police car in the first place—but then I remembered that he'd heard about my accident, and—anyhow, what did it matter? That was all over, and we were heading for a wonderful weekend.

I squeezed James's hand and said, "Off to the kitchen for me, darling. See you soon."

"But, darling—"

"Work before play," I said with mock severity, and went off to consult with Danny.

Emmy and Derek arrived about seven, and James entertained the Tibbett party in the bar (Reynolds sticking strictly to Perrier and lime), while I went about my usual duties. At my suggestion, he also joined them for dinner, as of course I could never sit down to a meal in my own dining room. I had a quick bite to eat before the first guests arrived, and then I was on duty until the last dish had been served; by which time I was able to join James, Derek, Henry, and Emmy at their table, where liqueurs (and another Perrier) were being served.

I asked Fred to bring me a Cointreau and raised it in a toast. "To my friends!" We all took a sip. Then, looking at James, I said, "And to my husband!"

Then Derek was off in the police car, and those two old married couples—the Tibbetts and the Gardiners—took themselves up to bed. I can't remember ever having been quite so happy.

CHAPTER

17

The next morning I was up early to supervise the usual hustle and bustle of arranging the buffet lunch in the garden. Danny, Pierre, and Mike were all in the kitchen before eight, preparing the cold dishes. I was out on the lawn watching Mr. Matthews and his helpers erecting the marquee, when James came out, looking worried. I went over to him at once.

"What's the matter, darling? You look grim."

"I feel grim."

"Why, James?"

"Oh, it's not all that terrible." He smiled at me. "It's just that I've had a call from London, and I have to go up to town at once."

"Oh, no, James! You can't! It's Saturday."

"I know it is, but business crises do sometimes arise on weekends, you know. I'll be back tomorrow."

"Not tonight?"

He squeezed my hand. "Tonight if I can make it," he promised. "Anyhow, I'm glad of one thing."

"What's that?"

"That Henry and Emmy are staying here. They'll be able to keep an eye on you."

"What do you mean, keep an eye?"

Very seriously James said, "That business with your car wasn't an accident, Susan. Somebody is out to harm you. I firmly believe it, and so does Henry."

I remembered Henry's warnings and shivered, although the day was already warm. I said, "Take care of yourself too, darling. If someone is out to hurt me, they might think about getting at you too."

James bent and kissed me, very gently. "Don't worry," he said. "We're a team now. We can lick anybody in the world."

"But your car. Supposing—"

"I've even thought of that, though I can't imagine how anybody could have tampered with it since yesterday. But to be on the safe side, I'll get Billy at the local garage to check it out before I go. Which is another reason I have to hurry. See you soon, angel."

It was just then that Daphne came out to tell me that Danny wanted to see me in the kitchen—something about smoked salmon that hadn't arrived—and by the time I had that sorted out, the Alfa had gone.

After that, things started their usual crescendo leading up to twelve o'clock, and I simply had no time to brood or worry. On the stroke of noon, everything was ready for our first guests. And you can imagine my surprise when they turned out to be a party of four, none other than Mr. Tredgold, complete with a mousy little woman in a floral print cotton dress, whom he introduced as his wife, and a rather good-looking middle-age couple—his son and daughter-in-law.

"You see, Miss Gardiner, I took you at your word," said Mr. Tredgold, twinkling away like the proverbial little star. "My word, what a difference in the old place. Wouldn't have Adam-and-Eved it, would you, Millie?" This to his wife.

"Makes me almost sorry I gave it up. But there, I just didn't have the time to devote to the old Moon, did I?" This to his son, on a somewhat apologetic note.

Strictly speaking, I could have turned them away, as they hadn't reserved and we were fully booked. But it was true that I had suggested they should come, and we can always squeeze in a few extra. So I motioned to Fred to find a nice table for the Tredgolds, and went about my business of greeting other guests.

Henry and Emmy had been over to Cregwell visiting the Manciples, but arrived back about half-past twelve. I made a beeline for their table.

Quietly I said into Henry's ear, "He's here. Tredgold. Look, over there. With his wife and family."

"So he is." Henry didn't sound very alarmed. "I'll keep an eye on him. Where's your old man?"

"James? He had to go to London on business."

"On a Saturday?"

"That's what I said. But apparently there's some crisis. Anyhow, he said he was glad that you were here to look after me. And so am I. I don't trust Tredgold."

Lunchtime peaked around half-past one. By half-past two most people were leaving, and no more arriving. I was tremendously busy, so I didn't actually see the Tredgolds go, but I noticed around half-past one that a new party had taken their table. Henry and Emmy lingered over coffee, and it must have been nearly two when I saw Daphne go over to their table. I didn't hear what was said, but Henry got up at once and followed her indoors, so I guessed it must be a telephone call.

Sure enough, a few minutes later he came out again and walked over to where I was speeding a parting couple and accepting their compliments. When they had gone off to their car, Henry said, "Well, Susan, I'm sorry, but I have to go the same way as James."

166

"Oh, Henry." I couldn't hide my disappointment. "You mean—back to London?"

"Afraid so. Crime doesn't take weekends off, you know."

"But Emmy will stay, won't she?"

He shook his head. "I doubt it. I'll have to take the car, and I shouldn't think she'd want to stay on without me."

"Well," I said, trying to be cheerful, "at least the Tredgolds have gone."

"Old man Tredgold hasn't," said Henry.

"What do you mean?"

"He's sitting in the bar on his own, drinking brandy."

"Oh, my God. Shall I get Daphne to tell him the bar's closing?"

"Don't bother," said Henry, looking over my shoulder to the door. "Here he comes now."

And so he did, making what seemed to me to be a rather unsteady way toward the car park. He stopped when he saw me and gave me a weak grin.

"Excellent, Miss G. Congratulate you. Just settling up my bill. My wife's driving home," he added, with a wary glance at Henry. "See you again soon." And he was off.

"Well, I'd better collect Emmy, pack our things, and get on the road," said Henry. He put his arm quickly round my shoulders and gave me a brief hug. "Don't worry. Will James be back this evening?"

"He said he would if he could, but—"

"Well, let's hope for the best. I must go now."

I felt distinctly desolate as I watched the Tibbetts' car driving away; but then I told myself not to be ridiculous. What could possibly happen? I was in my own home, with my own staff, and it was just an ordinary, busy Saturday. I went to my office and began reckoning up the takings.

By four o'clock the last of the lunchtime stragglers had left, and I went upstairs for a quick nap before starting to prepare for dinner. We had a healthy number of bookings and a fairly hectic evening to look forward to.

Hectic, but not in any way memorable. Danny had thought up a pretty sensational special—sliced breast of duck in cherry sauce with dauphiné potatoes, which was very popular. By half-past ten, however, the last diners were finishing their coffee and settling their bills. By half-past eleven, the washers-up were leaving the spotless kitchen, and Daphne brought me the beautifully kept account books, showing that it had been a highly profitable Saturday. She then shrugged on her coat, called "Good night," and went off in her little car to her lodgings in the village. In the silence that followed her departure, I realized that I was quite alone in The Blue Moon.

Well, there was nothing unusual about that. Night after night since we first opened I had spent on my own in the little inn and thought nothing of it. But now, somehow, everything was different.

Principally, of course, I was missing James. There had been no word from him, so I had no idea whether or not he was going to be able to get back that night. On an impulse, I went into Daphne's cubbyhole and telephoned his London apartment. The ringing tone went on monotonously, with no reply, not even from an answering machine. I couldn't make up my mind whether this was good or bad news. He might be on his way back to Danford already—but in that case, he surely would have switched on the answering machine. On the other hand, if his meeting (and, obviously, subsequent dinner) had gone on late enough, he might simply have started off for Essex straight from whatever restaurant he had dined at. I tried to remember whether or not we had left the machine on when we started off for Danford on Friday, but I couldn't. In fact, I couldn't even remember seeing the machine. Still hoping against hope that he would be back, I turned off the last of the lights, locked up, and went to bed.

I was woken by the insistent ringing of the front doorbell. Struggling against an enveloping sleep, I switched on the light. The clock beside my bed said 2:45 A.M.

My bedroom window overlooked the front door. I clambered out of bed, pulled on a dressing gown, ran to the window, and looked out. There was an unfamiliar black car in the drive, and a man standing at the door, his finger on the bell push.

He didn't seem to have noticed the light going on upstairs, so I called down, "Who is it? What do you want?"

He looked up, but his face was shaded by a broad-brimmed hat and impossible to recognize on this moonless night. The only thing I felt sure of was that it wasn't Mr. Tredgold. This man was too tall. A voice with a slight Cockney tinge in it said, "Mrs. Gardiner?"

Mrs. Gardiner? How many people knew about my marriage? Very few. I was sure this wasn't one of them.

"Yes. What is it?"

"Please come down. I've some rather bad news, I'm afraid."

"Who are you?"

"Police, madam."

"Oh, my God! Wait, I'm coming!"

I fairly flew down the stairs. All the nameless and formless fears that I had had all day now crystallized into certainty. Something terrible had happened to James.

All right, I know I was foolish. I should have considered quietly and calmly, that somebody would have telephoned me first. I didn't think of anything like that. I just thought of James. And that is why, about half a minute later, when I opened the front door, I found myself face to face with Montague.

"Montague! What on earth?"

He sort of hesitated for a moment, then grabbed me by the arm. Hard. "You're coming with me."

"Oh, Montague, don't be silly. Where?"

"Where I say."

He was stronger than I would have thought. He was pulling me toward the river. I fought back as best I could, but we were already very close to the bank, when he suddenly put his face very close to mine and whispered, "Miss Susan, he's in the car!"

"Who is?" I whispered back.

"Why, of course—"

"What should I do?" So Tredgold was in the car, and Montague had mysteriously become my ally. He gave my cheek an encouraging pat. "Just lie still and slip into the river. I'm supposed to have knocked you out."

I relaxed in Montague's arms and let him push me down into the water. And then I heard the most wonderful sound in the world. James's voice, urgent and tense.

"What the hell is going on here?" And then, "Susan! Where are you, Susan?"

Rising bubbling to the surface, like Clementine, I shouted, "Here, James!"

The next thing I knew, James was wading into the river and had me in his arms.

He said, "Oh, Susan, I'm so sorry . . ." And then I couldn't breathe, and everything went black, blacker than any night I had ever known.

18

I woke up very slowly. It was daylight, and I was lying in my own bed. As I opened my eyes, the first thing I saw was Emmy's face. She was sitting on a chair beside the bed, reading. As soon as I stirred, she put down her book and smiled at me.

"Welcome back, Susan," she said.

Gradually recollection began to come back. I tried to struggle up into a sitting position. I remembered now. The river. Montague. James. "Where's James?"

Gently Emmy pushed me back down on the bed.

"You have to rest, Susan. You had a very narrow escape."

"Where's James?" I was trying to shout, but I couldn't get out more than a sort of kitten's squeak, and my throat hurt abominably.

Emmy stood up. "Just rest for the moment, Susan." She walked to the door, and I saw her push the bell that rang downstairs. "Dr. Trumper is here. He'll be right up to see you. Henry and Derek too."

This time I did manage to sit up. "Something's happened to James, and you won't tell me!" I croaked.

Emmy turned slowly to look at me. Her face was calm and very sad. She said, "Yes, Susan. Something has happened." She came over, sat on the bed, and took my hand. "I know this is going to be terribly difficult for you to understand, Susan. James is in prison."

"In prison!"

She squeezed my hand. "My dear, he tried to kill you. Twice. That's something you're going to have to accept, and learn to live with."

"You're lying!"

"Oh, Susan, I wish I was."

Then the door opened, and Dr. Trumper came in, followed by Henry. Emmy said simply, "I've told her. I had to."

"You shouldn't have, Mrs. Tibbett." The doctor sounded really angry.

"She deserved to know, for God's sake," said Emmy.

They faced each other, full of hostility. Henry said, "My wife is right, Doctor. Susan might have imagined something worse."

"There couldn't be anything worse," I said. "It's a pack of lies. Don't you understand? It was Montague—and then James came to save me—"

Henry and the doctor exchanged a long look. Then Henry said, "I'm not going to explain to you now, Susan. The doctor says you have to sleep, and he's going to give you a shot to help you do just that. Later on, I promise you, I'll tell you everything."

I managed to say, "What are you doing to James?"

"Nothing. He's answering some questions, that's all."

The doctor was preparing a syringe, and I turned to Henry in panic. "Henry! You're lying to me!"

Henry shook his head. "Have I ever lied to you, Susan?"

"I'm not so sure."

"That's better. That's more like Susan Gardiner. Now have a good sleep. And please trust me."

I felt a faint pricking in my arm, and then no more.

The next time I woke, it had to be evening, because the curtains were drawn and the lights were on. Emmy was still sitting patiently by my bedside.

She smiled. "How are you feeling now, Susan?"

"I feel O.K. A bit weak. My throat seems to be better."

"The doctor says you should have something light to eat. I'll get the kitchen to send something up. What would you like?"

"Nothing. What time is it?"

Emmy glanced at her watch. "Half-past eight. Now, what shall I tell Danny to prepare?"

"I don't want any food," I said. "I want to see James. There's obviously been some awful misunderstanding—"

Emmy shook her head. "I'm afraid there hasn't."

"Well, Henry promised me he'd explain. Where's Henry?"

"He's downstairs. Do you feel up to seeing him?"

"Of course I do."

"Now, don't try to sit up. Just rest quietly, and I'll get him."

She went out of the room, and was back a couple of minutes later. "He's coming up. He's bringing your supper."

"I told you I didn't want anything."

"The doctor says—"

"Damn and blast the doctor!"

Emmy sighed. "Well, I can't force-feed you. But do try, Susan."

I glared at her, and then rolled over on the bed so that my back was toward her. And that's how I was when Henry came in with the tray.

Danny had certainly done his best. There was homemade consommé, poached salmon trout with hollandaise sauce, a

173

few tiny new potatoes, and fresh peas. Everything simple and delicious. And a red rose from the garden tucked into the crisp white damask table napkin. It was the sight of that tray, so lovingly prepared, that finally got to me, I suppose. Anyhow, I suddenly found myself in floods of tears, burying my head furiously in my pillow to smother the ugly, rasping sobs.

Henry put the tray down, came over, and sat on the bed. He touched my shoulder gently. "That's right, Susan. Have a good cry. You'll feel much better."

And do you know, he was quite right. As my fit of weeping died down, I felt drained—drained of anger, drained of hope. But calm.

"Now," said Henry, almost cheerfully, "have something to eat. And we can talk."

Emmy plumped my pillows and helped me to sit up and take the bowl of soup in both hands. I sipped it slowly as Henry talked.

"It's a long story, Susan. And not a pretty one. You must be prepared for that."

I nodded, between sips.

"Well, it started even before you inherited The Blue Moon. James had been sailing very close to the wrong side of big finance. I know now that the Fraud Squad had had its eyes on him for some time."

"Whatever for?"

"Insider trading. Using privileged knowledge to make a personal fortune. I'm afraid it's almost like a disease. With some people, the more money they get, the more they must have. Nothing else means anything. Those are the people called misers."

"But James spent so generously—"

"Only in order to make more. You remember John H. Deitweiler? The American?"

"Yes, I do. I didn't like him."

"No more do I," Henry agreed, "but that's neither here nor there. The fact is that he is an extremely high-powered financier from New York. And for over a year he has been negotiating to arrange for the building of a big American automobile factory here in England. Here in Danford, to be exact. The scheme, which has just been finalized, is to build a road bridge over the Dan connecting the site with the main London road.

"The site of the factory will consist of that derelict property next door, which James bought without trouble some time ago—and The Blue Moon and its land. This property, Susan, is a gold mine. Its owner will be able to name his own price."

Something suddenly came back to me. "So that's what he meant!"

"What who meant?"

"Deitweiler. When he was lunching here, he made a curious remark about something being a pity. James passed it off, but it obviously referred to the fact that The Blue Moon was going to be bulldozed to make way for a ruddy car factory."

"Well, I don't know about that," said Henry, "but I do know that James was already plotting with Deitweiler to get hold of this site. He'd been making discreet inquiries to find out who the owner was. Imagine his reaction when he found that it had belonged to his great-uncle Sebastian, and that you were the new proprietor."

"You mean—that's why he came down here with me the first time? And why he knew the way, when I didn't?"

"Of course."

"And he tried to buy it off me, that very day," I exclaimed.

"Did he, now? I didn't know that, of course. But it must have been a great shock when he found that you were a trained restaurateur, and intended to keep the place, restore it, and get it running again. Not part of his plan at all."

"You're not saying that he fixed for those people to be killed, Henry!"

"I'm afraid so, Susan. When he found that he couldn't get you out any other way, he decided to try to scare you out. And if you hadn't been such a stubborn lady, he would probably have succeeded. I was convinced almost from the beginning that your poor guests who were poisoned were picked entirely at random. They both had the misfortune to order the final helping of a special dish with mushrooms in it."

"So he was working through Montague?"

"That's right. It was James who got him to answer that advertisement of yours. Montague is not a countryman, and even though you had told him about the Destroying Angel, he didn't recognize it the first time James brought it to him and told him to mix it in the food, He thought it was some kind of practical joke. Well, that's his story, and we can't disprove it. After Miss Fotheringay's death, of course, Montague could be blackmailed into doing it again. No wonder he was trying to get away. But in the end he did the sensible thing. He came to me."

"So he never really disappeared?"

"I knew where he was," Henry said shortly. "Well, as we all know, in spite of two murders, The Blue Moon didn't fail. Thanks to you and Danny and Daphne, it began doing better than ever. And the final date for the factory agreement was getting very near. There was only one thing for James to do. Marry you and kill you. Then he'd be undisputed owner of this property."

I trembled, spilling some of the soup.

Henry went on, "I have to be absolutely frank with you, Susan. I was gradually building up my evidence against James, hoping to be sure enough of my facts to arrest him—when Emmy called me with the terrible news that you had married him."

"I don't know how you can be sure of all this," I said.

"It was he who sabotaged your car, while it was in his garage in London," Emmy put in.

"But Tredgold—"

"That was a subtle touch," said Henry. "He knew you would stop at that particular filling station—it's the only one for miles. He arranged for Tredgold to be there, and to act suspiciously."

"How could he possibly have done that?"

"Very simple. Tredgold's company hasn't been paying taxes as it should, and James knew it. So he was in a position to dictate. Susan, you have to realize that his whole relationship with you was a sham. Even that apartment that he took you to—that's not where he really lives."

"I did think it was—well, impersonal."

"As soon as I heard the address you had given the police after your accident, I knew. He rented it just for a week or two. His real home is in the same neighborhood—but of course he couldn't take you there, because he doesn't live alone."

I was past surprise. "He's married?"

"Only to you," Henry said grimly. "But he's been living with his girlfriend for the past seven years. You remember Sylvia—the very pretty girl who was at that hotel with him?"

"Was that why you were there?"

"Partly. She was in on the scheme, of course. She would have had her share of the loot. Emmy and I got down here as soon as we could to try to protect you—but as soon as I heard that James was going to London on Saturday, I knew he had decided to act. That's why I had to make sure that Tredgold—who was spying for James—overheard my bogus telephone conversation with Derek. I knew he would report that Emmy and I were leaving and that the coast was clear. Of course, we didn't go far. Derek's phone call was actually to tell me that Montague had reported to him that he'd been summoned for duty last night." Henry paused and smiled. "It's Derek you should really be grateful to. He was first on the scene, and it was he who knocked James out when he was strangling you under the water."

"James didn't . . . ?"

"I'm afraid so." Henry was apologetic. "You see, in spite of Montague turning Queen's Evidence, we had to catch him in the act. I'm terribly sorry, Susan."

"That's what he said—James, I mean," I said bitterly. I put down the soup bowl and took off the diamond ring and the wedding band. "Will you give these back to James for me? I won't be needing them."

Henry smiled, a wry smile. "I'll give them back to the jeweler who was foolish enough to let them go with only a deposit and a credit card. They were never paid for, and would never have been."

After I had eaten, I went to sleep again. Dr. Trumper's sedatives were certainly strong. I woke up just as the first fingers of light were pushing through the gap in the curtains. There was a big, reassuring figure sitting in the chair by the bed.

"Who's that?" I murmured, still half asleep.

"It's Derek, Susan. Sitting in for Emmy for a few hours."

Before I knew it, I was asleep again. When I surfaced once more, Derek was murmuring something softly to himself. Something about someone called Andy, and what a marvel he was. I didn't open my eyes. He went on, very quietly, "Had we but world enough and time, this coyness, lady, were no crime . . ."

Drowsiness closed in again, but next time I woke, he was murmuring something about dragging our pleasures with rough strife through the iron gates of life. I opened my eyes, and he stopped abruptly.

I didn't realize until a lot later on exactly what I had been hearing. I told you I never got farther than O levels, and English literature was not my hottest subject. But I did realize that I was listening to a totally different Derek Reynolds from the gruff individual that I had known.

I held out my hand. "Thank you," I said. "For everything." He took it in his large, friendly paw, and I realize now that I must have drifted off to sleep still clutching it, because when Daphne came in with my breakfast tray, Derek and I were still holding hands.

EPILOGUE

A month later, I was sitting at one of my own buffet lunch tables on the lawn with Henry, Derek, Emmy, and old Mr. Prothero—who had aged visibly since the first time I met him in his office. It was not so much a council of war as a cabinet meeting. On the table was a letter from one of the biggest American car manufacturers (their legal department, actually) containing a ridiculously enormous offer for The Blue Moon and its land, with a subtle hint that they might go even higher if pressed.

James was in prison, awaiting trial, and I had started divorce proceedings. Montague and Tredgold were both ready to testify against him. The question before the meeting was, what to do about the American offer.

I was in a minority of one. I stated my case.

"I've worked like a dog to make a success of this place. I honestly don't feel like starting all over again somewhere else. Besides, I like it here."

Prothero said, "You'll never get another offer like this, Mrs. . . . em . . . Ms. Gardiner. You'd be mad not to take it."

Henry said, "This inn has such unhappy memories, Susan. First, you uncle's poor wife. Then—everything else . . ."

Emmy said, "You could always take over The Golden Goose. Jack Pargeter won't be back for a long time."

"All the same—"

Derek said to Prothero, "Would that amount of money be enough to start a restaurant in London?"

"Of course. And with plenty to spare."

"Because," Derek said, "I certainly don't intend to resign from the C.I.D., so after we're married we'll have to live in London."

I looked at him. "Is that a proposal?"

"Of course it is, idiot."

"And I could bring Daphne and Danny and Pierre and Mike and Fred—"

"Anybody you like."

"Quite a small place, maybe somewhere near the river, like Chiswick or Barnes?"

"Why not?"

"All right," I said, "I accept."

Prothero raised his eyebrows. "Both offers?"

I held out my hand to Derek. "Of course."